Meghadutam

Translated into English in vers libre

BY

ASHOK KUMAR JHA

PARTRIDGE

A Penguin Random House Company

To order additional copies of this book, contact
Toll Free 800 101 2657 (Singapore)
Toll Free 1 800 81 7340 (Malaysia)
orders.singapore@partridgepublishing.com

www.partridgepublishing.com/singapore

In memory of my father who loved reciting verses
from this poem in Sanskrit

Contents

Preface

The Meghaduta, no less than his *Shakuntala*, has attracted steady attention from among the Kalidasan texts in the West. As such both native Indian and some western readers of this poem in Sanskrit have been drawn to it in an attempt to render it in translation for an English knowing reading public in India and abroad. That the poem was able to draw the attention of readers in Germany, England and elsewhere speaks of the power of Kalidasa's imagination at its best in expression in poetry in classical Sanskrit. A prose translation of it in a European language may not be able to communicate the music of his words or the picturesque appeal of his images in the author's own language, but it may be able all the same to present something of the ingenuity and structural design in verbal organisation he had in mind in that language.

The modern European languages into which this poem was translated are analytical in character. So the translators in them did not have the tools to capture the great power of verbal synthesis which accounts for something of the charm of the poem in Sanskrit, besides the usual advantage of inspiration and a conception of the structural design that the first poet has.

A classic in paraphrase is an unenviable preoccupation as it must fall short of the richness and adequacy of expression in the original. But even such attempts have helped to keep an interest in Kalidasa alive in the modern world.

Translations, hence, of this great work have varied in merit. H. H. Wilson, F. Max Muller, M. R. Kale, Pt. Sitaram Chaturvedi and Janardan Shastri Pandey tried their hands at translating *The Meghaduta* into languages separated from Sanskrit by vast stretches of time and space.

H. H. Wilson in his verse translation of the poem tried to capture the poetic ethos of the text in English in the available diction of poetry in his time. His diction is a version of the mid-nineteenth century poetic diction current in English when he made this effort. There are worthwhile patches of versification in his work, but it is obvious that with the kind of verbal equipment that he has in his text, it was difficult for him to communicate the actual appeal of the poem either with respect to its music or the indigenous character of the poem's imagery. In fact, rhetoric and poetry in such versification seems to interfere with a fanciful representation of the Kalidasan text in a language which has moved away from inflectional propensities to become an analytical language at last.

I tried, therefore, to translate *The Meghaduta* in vers libre, which may be of help to us to see it closer to what is of value to us in much of the poetry of our time. The excellent work carried out by Ezra Pound in this respect in re-creating Chinese poetry in English in the twentieth century may be a pointer in this direction. We may hope to retrieve something of the original spirit of Kalidasan poetry in a translation in free verse to come back to a possible response to the originality of a great poet which it is difficult for the modern reader to come to unless, of course, he goes through the labour of acquiring a knowledge of Sanskrit itself.

27. 1. 2013
Patna

THE MEGHADUTA
Canto One

Purva Meghah

(Advent of the First Cloud)

I

Love-sick and engrossed with himself,
Neglectful of his duties,
A *Yaksha* was deprived of his position and
    asked to live in exile,
Away from his wife and abode for a year.
He came then, to spend his days under a thick
    canopy of trees at *Ramagiri Ashrama,* where
Janaki used to perform her ablutions in tanks
    and fountains once.

II

One who could not live apart from her even for
    a moment,
Who had become so thin, pining after his love,
That his gold bangles came off his hands,
That lover came to spend a few months there.
But on the very first day of *Asadha* could he see
A patch of clouds moving over the hill in front,
As if an elephant were at play,
Stooping, butting against a hillock with his
    head.

*Note: Italicised words and phrases explained
in the notes at the end of the book.*

3

III

Standing in front of it, somehow,
Eager, given to longing,
Obedient to his overlord,
He suppressed his tears, remaining absorbed
    for a while.
A patch of cloud stirs us.
What about one who has been separated from
    his beloved!

IV

Clouds nearby made him think of her,
She may be pining for him.
"Shouldn't I send a message of my well-being
    to her
With this patch of a passing cloud?" he
    thought.
He took some *Kutuja* flowers and welcomed the
    patch in front of him, eager and prayerful.

V

A message can be conveyed by one
Who is subtle and cognizant of what it implies.
While this patch of cloud was made of
Mere smoke, light, wind and water;
But, like many given to desire in love,
He could not distinguish between the living and
    the non-living.
Oblivious of what it was,
He prayed to the cloud.

VI

"I know you belong to the famous race of
    clouds of *Pushkara* and *Avartaka,*
And that you convey messages for the *overlord
    of gods*
Changing your form at will!
Hence it is, I entreat you,
Live as I do, apart from my life's companion.
Addressed to a person of merit,
Though without consequence,
A request is still worth itself,
Better than a gainful bid with the degenerate.

VII

"Dear you are, and a refuge
To those afflicted with summer heat,
As also love.
Go therefore, with a message from me,
To her, my love,
Who has been separated from me by the *lord
of riches*.
Go to *Alaka*, the dwelling place of the princely
Yakshas;
There, the mansions remain lit by the crescent
moon on *Shiva's* head, in its outer garden.

VIII

"As you ride upon the wind's path,
Women who have their husbands travelling
abroad
Will look at you,
Holding up their tresses,
Hoping they may be coming.
But for mine who knows how I depend for a
living on another,
What man, living far from his home,
Would not be expected!

IX

"Eager, my wife must be counting days,
    brother!
Go, unimpeded to her,
She is still alive.
Hope sustains the heart of a woman,
For it is tender like a flower
And full of love.

X

"Slow blows a favourable wind for you,
And a *Chataka* tunes a vibrant note,
Knowing the glad moment of conception has
    come,
Cranes fly in rows across the sky;
They would fan your beauteous shapes with
    their wings all the way.

XI

"Mushrooms begin to sprout with your
    reverberations,
And the earth becomes fertile, gathering
    moisture from the air;
Longing to go to *Lake Manas*,
The royal swans too are joyous to hear the
    sound of thunder.
With the lotus-stalks in their beaks, for passage
    fare to *Mount Kailasha*,
They will go with you along.

XII

"Take leave of him,
After you have embraced this lofty mountain,
    dear friend,
Who has the *footprints of Rama on his slopes*.
Time alone could make you meet him,
For you are able to meet him after a long
    separation
That makes him shed hot tears.

XIII

"Hear from me first about the path as I depict it
 to you,
You may then listen to a message agreeable to
 your ear.
Fatigued with setting your feet from peak to
 peak, and spent up,
You should
Take water from fountains on the way from time
 to time.

XIV

"Go up in the sky with your face turned to the
 north
From this place overgrown with canes,
With the naïve consorts of the *Siddhas*
Looking at you with wonder in their eyes:
Was a gale carrying away the mountain top?
Flying so, you would push aside
The thick uplifted trunks of huge tuskers
As you go north.

XV

"There, above the anthill,
The rainbow fragment would look lovely,
Like a mixed lot of precious stones.
And your dark body would charm the eye,
As if it was *Krishna* standing there,
And his head was crowned with peacock
    feathers.

XVI

"Innocent peasant women will look up, curious
As products on their farms
Depend on your coming.
There, in the *Mala* lands,
You must rain as the soil is upturned with the
    plough,
And one breathes the earth-smell.
Go west hence,
Then turn to the north.

XVII

"For extinguishing the fire in its jungles with
    your showers,
Amrakuta will have you on its top,
Where you can rest awhile,
For you would be tired journeying so far.
Not even those placed low in life,
Conscious of favours done to them,
Turn their back upon their benefactors,
When they come to them for shelter in need,
Not to speak of the privileged.

XVIII

"With you placed on its head,
Like a dark braid of beautiful hair,
And groves of yellowish ripe mangoes below,
The mountain may strike one to be the breast
    of earth;
Dark at the centre and fair below,
A sight the divine pairs may like to watch from
    above.

XIX

"O Cloud! When you reach the peak of
    Amrakuta, tired,
Rain down the summer fires in its woods with
    your showers;
For those who have attained a measure of
    eminence
Do not forget to give back something in return.

XX

"Stay awhile where the forest women move
    between the hedges,
And move on,
Because, emptied of water, you can move more
    quickly.
Here you can see *Reva*, broken up in several
    streams
By the uneven mountain terrain of the *Vindhyas*
That looks like a huge dark tusker,
Its body painted with lines of ash.

XXI

"After showers there,
You could drink from *Reva's* waters,
Full of the smell of the wild elephants that bathe
    in it,
And the blackberry trees as the river passes
    through them.
When you have such substance,
You cannot be wafted by a mere wind.
Light is a person devoid of substance,
While those who have enough, get their due.

XXII

"You will see bees hovering over
Ripe orange-red *Kadamba* petals,
The dear grazing *Kandali* leaves on marshy river
    banks,
And elephants smelling the sharp scent of the
    wild forest earth.
They would show you the path.

XXIII

"You will find consorts of the *Siddhas*,
Looking high up with wonder at how a *Chataka*
Catches at rain drops
And counting cranes flying one by one.
And their partners will be grateful to you,
As surprised by the sudden sound of thunder,
These ladies may in fear embrace them for the
    moment.

XXIV

"I know, O friend! You want to serve my cause,
But I would like you to linger awhile on those
    mountains
Fragrant with the flowering *Kutuja*;
There peacocks will greet you with tears of joy
    in their eyes.
I hope you to travel fast still all the same.

XXV

"Close to the *Dasharna* country
You will find hedges surrounding the gardens
White with flowering *Ketakis* at their apex,
And noisy birds nesting in the sacred trees in
   villages.
The forest skirts them with dark *Jamun* trees
   with ripe fruits,
And there may be some swans too.
Come to rest there for a while.

XXVI

"There, as you reach *Vidisha,*
Its famous capital,
You will obtain at once
What you desire most.
When you strike with the sound of thunder by
   the banks of *Vetrawati,*
You could drink water from its ripples.
It may be like drinking the sap from the lips,
Which lie beneath the arch eyebrows of a lovely
   woman.

XXVII

"You should rest for a while then on *Nichai*,
A hill, where *Kadamba* will break into flowers at
  your touch,
There you will smell perfumes coming of the
  mountain caves.
This will remind you of how wanton youths,
Sons of the rich of the city,
Come here with courtesans to have good time.

XXVIII

"Resting there awhile, move on.
Shower drops of fresh water on jasmines in the
  gardens on the river banks.
Cast your shadow there over girls plucking
  flowers.
Some broken lotus petals stick to their sweating
  cheeks.
Have a few words of good cheer with them,
And pass on.

XXIX

"You should go, though it is not straight,
Over the road to *Ujjain*,
And see tall palaces that belong to that city.
You may direct many a playful glance
Watching the women in that city;
Or you are deceived of the sense behind living.
Surprised by the sudden flash of lightning
    around you,
They will cast arched glances at you.

XXX

"With a row of noisy birds over turbulent waves,
Stumbling, then gliding with grace,
Nirvindhya shows its navel in eddies.
You must partake of her water,
For a woman invites her lover with a gesture.

XXXI

"Beyond it, O Fortunate One! You will see her
    undistracted current of water
Looking like one braid, and the *Sindhu* appears
    pale due to the fallen leaves on its banks.
You should act in a manner she is propitiated.

XXXII

"You will reach then *Avanti*,
Where village elders will tell you the story of
    Udayana
And that prospering city called *Vidisha*
I told you about earlier.
There, it appears, when the outcome of their
    deeds of virtue is spent in heaven, the
    illustrious dead return.

XXXIII

"There, the cranes prolong
Their sweet carousal in the early morning,
And a breeze bears the sweet smell of the
    lotuses in *Shipra*.
It relieves the lovelorn ladies of the labours of
    their love.
Like the sweet prattle of a persuasive lover and
    his gestures,
It soothes them in fatigue.

XXXIV

"And there, in the market, you will see
Numerous pearl-necklaces with a precious
    stone as their central gem,
Conches, pearl shells, emerald gems
Dark-green, like green grass,
With their rays deflected outward,
And corals arranged for sale,
So many, you will feel
The sea has only water left in it.

XXXV

"There you will meet people telling unknowing
    kinfolks,
Who have come from afar,
How king of the *Vatsa* country
Took away the dear daughter of *Pradyota*,
And it was here that the king had a garden of
    golden *Tala* trees.
Here roamed *Nalagiri*, his elephant,
After he uprooted his tie-post;
Gone mad, he was in great fury.

XXXVI

"Incense smoke coming out of the windows
   there
Will make you appear bigger.
The peacocks would take you to be a kin,
And dance when they see you.
Relax for a while in that city of flowers and
   mansions,
Where the raw imprint of the coloured
   footsteps of
The lovely women who live in them can still be
   seen.

XXXVII

"You should visit then, that sacred abode of the
   Lord of Chandi and the three worlds.
There his followers will gaze at you,
For you have the same complexion as the
   colour of his neck.
There you will feel a wind blowing from
   Gandhawati
That carries the sweet smell of the scents of
   lotuses in it and bathing women.

XXXVIII

"O Cloud! If you reach the temple of *Mahakala*
     before time,
Wait till the sun sets.
And when the evening prayer of *Shiva* begins,
Strike your drums deep.
Such a moderate voice of thunder in his honour
Will get for you the fruit one craves for.

XXXIX

"With jingling bells in their anklets,
And their hands tired of holding fly-whisks
     studded with gems,
Their limbs with cuts and nail-marks,
The dancing girls will cast long side glances at
     you, grateful for a relief.
Their glances may appear to be a flight of bees.
They will be grateful to you for your cool and
     soothing showers.

XL

"While the evening prayer is done,
And the *Lord himself starts dancing,*
You should hang over the trees,
That will appear to be his lifted arms.
In the crimson light of the sunset,
He will appear to have an elephant's hide over
    his shoulders.
Afraid at first, his consort will
Gaze at you more intently afterward,
Finding you so devoted to her lord.
He is also the Lord of all living beings.

XLI

"In nights pitch-dark, when nothing can be seen
    on roads,
When women in love go out to meet their
    lovers,
Show them the path,
Like a streak of gold on the touchstone,
With a flash of lightning,
With no reverberation of thunder or rain,
For it may confuse them.

XLII

"Quite fatigued with her flashes,
Heavy with her surcharge,
You must spend the night with her,
Over the thatch of a house,
That has a pair of pigeons nesting in its eaves.
Set on your course again as soon as the sun is
    out,
For those who want to help their friends,
Do not like to slow down.

XLIII

"You should not obstruct the sun with your
    body in the way,
He may take it ill.
For, on his return then,
He has to wipe the dew drops on lotuses with
    his rays.
After he has been out for the night,
He returns, as some lovers do,
Who come back to their unhappy wives;
He would try to placate them and beguile them.

XLIV

"When the shadow of your dark shape will fall
Over the water in *Gambhira*, the river below,
You can see your true self in it,
As the water in it is as pure as consciousness
　　itself.
White as flowers, move the rapid, noisy fish in it;
That you may take to be the love glances of a
　　woman.

XLV

"As if held by a hand, the cane thicket,
Touches the river water,
Slipping like a blue garment down her hips.
Still bent upon her,
After you have sipped her drink,
Enjoying a good deal of its contents till the
　　banks show out,
You may find it difficult to move ahead.
What man who has the experience can turn
　　away from the loins of a woman?

XLVI

"A cool breeze bearing smell of the earth after
    your showers,
Will help the figs to ripen,
While the elephants will inhale it,
And produce curious sounds.
Move on to *Dewagiri* with the gentle breeze.

XLVII

"There you should wash *Skanda* with your
    showers.
Born of the god who has the young moon on
    his head
From the mouth of *Agni* he came to protect the
    army of gods.
Sprinkle drops of *Ganga* water,
As if they are petals of flowers, upon him;
For the river flows through heaven first before it
    comes down.

XLVIII

"Afterwards, prolong the reverberating sound
Of your thunder in the mountains;
Make *Skanda's* peacock dance,
A corner of his eyes reflecting light from *Shiva's*
    moon;
Its fallen feathers still bear circular streaks of
    lustre
That *Bhavani* places on her ears instead of
    flowers.

XLIX

"After you have paid homage to *Skanda*, the
    god of war,
You will meet the *Siddhas* lute-in hand with
    their wives,
They will turn away from you
In fear of getting drenched with rain drops.
Stop there and hang down over *Charmawati*,
Sipping its water, in obeisance to *Rantideva's*
    glory,
As it was the outcome of his great sacrificial
    rites to honour the gods.

L

"When you will bend down to drink water from
  the river,
Looking dark, *a counterfeit of Vishnu,*
The ranging *Siddhas* and *Gandharvas* will look
  at you intently.
Down below, you will appear like a precious
  blue stone pendant,
And the river will look like a necklace around
  the earth's neck.

LI

"Go then to *Dashpur* across *Charmawati,*
Turning your beauteous shape, an object worth
  attention
For the long, dark eyelashes of the ladies of
  Dashpur,
Moving up and down over eyes,
Where red and white alternate
Like dark bees over flowering *Kundas.*

LII

"Moving over *Brahmavarta*, you will go to
    Kurukshetra,
Where *Arjuna* who bore the *Gandiva*,
Shot down his numerous opponents with
    arrows
As the rain drops you shower on lotuses.

LIII

"Like *Balarama* who chose not to fight on any
    side in the *Great War*
Who would rather drink the pure water of
    Saraswati
Reflecting the intoxication of liquor in *Rewati's*
    eyes,
You should then partake of her water.
That would purify your soul, though you look
    dark outside.

LIV

"Thence you will go to *Kankhal,*
Where you will meet *Jahnu's* daughter,
Who proved to be a flight of steps to heaven for
 Sagara's sons.
The white foam on its waves might appear to
 be making fun
Of the frown on *Gauri's* face,
As she comes to reach across and seize *Shiva's*
 hair,
The hand of her waves touching the moon on
 his head.

LV

"If you think of drinking her transparent water,
Like an elephant from the heavenly quarters,
Suspended from above by your hinder parts,
Your dusky image will be reflected in the
 moving stream along.
The river will take on a beauteous look,
Like the one effected downstream in a union
 with *Yamuna* at *Prayaga.*

LVI

"Being tired, you will rest on the mountain peak
    awhile;
Which, white with snow and scented as the
    musk dear squat thereon,
Is the source of the river.
There, you will look like the mud on the head of
    Shiva's bull.

LVII

"O Cloud! When there is fire in the forest,
As there is friction between deodars in a storm,
And the hairy yaks get singed in their tails,
Rain it down with your showers.
This is how the bountiful rich like to alleviate the
    affliction of the poor.

LVIII

"If the *Sharabhas* jump at hearing the sound of
    thunder,
Let rain hail on them,
And scatter them.
For truants who go in for pranks
Deserve to be corrected after all.

LIX

"There on the *Himvanta* you will find a footprint
   of the god with the crescent moon on his
   head.
It is worshipped by the *Siddhas.*
If you go round it in humility,
You may be absolved of your sins
And become one of his *ganas* after death.

LX

"There the wind passing through
Thickets of hollow bamboos produce musical
   notes,
While *Kinnara* women sing in chorus of the
   triumph over *Tripura.*
If your thunder resounding then in the caves,
Will be as deep as the beat of a tabor,
Such music will integrate all the aspects of
   Shiva's symphony.

LXI

"Crossing those scenes unique to the mountain,
You should pass on sideways through that
     passage
Carved out by *Parashurama* with his arrow
Like a hole such as the flamingos live in.
It is a gateway to the swans now.
Elongated, going through it sideways,
Your length extended,
You will look comely like the extended foot of
     Vishnu
Who tried to measure *Bali's* claim to eminence
     for the sake of gods.

LXII

"You should rise a little higher and be the guest
     of *Mount Kailasha*,
Whose joints were loosened by *Ravana*.
It serves now as a mirror to the consorts of the
     gods.
Touching the skies with its peaks,
It is, as it were, the loud laugh of *Shiva*
     accumulated day by day.

LXIII

"Looking black like kohl, powdered and glossy,
You should, I hope, rest on the skirt of the
    mountain looking white like ivory.
It will be a beautiful sight for the eyes to look
    upon,
As if the plough-bearer has a dark tunic over his
    shoulders.

LXIV

"And so that *Gauri* may have his hand,
Shiva would lay off the serpent around it,
As they climb the pleasant mountain slope.
Harden yourself into a flight of steps for her,
It will help her to go up the gem-studded path
    to the peak.

LXV

"Pricking you with the hard points of their
    bracelets,
The sweet maidens of heaven will make you rain
    water,
They would like to turn you into a shower bath.
If, then, dear friend, you cannot procure your
    release
When it is hot,
You should beat the drum of your thunder hard
    to scare them.

LXVI

"Covering the face of *Airavata* with that delicate
    and thin film,
Which you have for the time being,
Take your drink from *Lake Manas*, full of golden
    lotuses,
And make the *Kalpa* tree sprout with your
    breeze.
With these and some other sportive actions, O
    Cloud!
You should make your stay worthwhile over that
    mountain peak.

LXVII

"O form that shapes itself as per its will! It is not
   that you
Cannot tell that city with the *Ganga* dropping
   from it,
Like a woman who sits on the lap of her lover
   with her garments in disorder.
Lying on the slope of the mountain,
With its tall mansions, *Alaka* can keep up
A multitude of clouds showering rain drops,
Like a woman arranging her tresses interwoven
   with pearls.

Canto Two

Uttara Meghah

(The Cloud Later)

I

"O Cloud! That city with its mansions can
   compare to you.
You have flashy lightning,
While the mansions there have beauties bright;
You have a picturesque rainbow,
While they have paintings of varied colours,
   hanging on their walls,
You give out deep and pleasant rumbles,
While they have their tabors beaten for music;
You have watery interiors,
They have floors paved with sapphires;
And if you rise high in the firmament,
They have domes that touch the sky.

II

"Young married women play there with lotuses
   wrapped around their hands,
Have their hair interwoven with fresh *Kunda*
   blossoms,
Their face powdered with the yellow-white
   pollen of *Lodharas*,
They put on fresh *Kurbaka* blooms in their
   braids and *Nipa* petals on the parting line of
   their hair.

III

"There are trees there,
Full of flowers ever,
And you will find bees hovering over them.
There are lotuses surrounded by swans
    throughout the year.
And domestic peacocks with resplendent
    plumage given to shrill shrieks with upraised
    necks,
And the nights have their darkness removed by
    the moon,
That is pleasant and bright.

IV

"There, the *Yakshas* know only tears of bliss,
No torment, save that caused by the arrows of
    Kamadeva.
This can, of course, be disabled when the lovers
    meet.
There is no separation for them save perhaps
    from love quarrels,
And there is no other age than youth.

V

"When the *Yakshas* pass their time with
   beauties on wassail grounds,
Adjacent to their houses paved with precious
   crystal,
They look as if they are decorated with flowers,
While they keep on drinking a love-stirring
   liquor,
Coming of the *wish-granting trees,*
Where there is a beat of drums,
Quite like your gentle rumbles.

VI

"There in the golden sands by the side of the
   cool *Mandakini* under *Mandara* trees,
The girls sought for marriage even by the gods,
Hide jewels with one hand and seek them with
   another.

VII

"Ashamed, with the knot of their garment
    loosened by the quick moving hands of their
    lovers,
Those women of scarlet lips,
Throw a handful of scented powder at the gem-
    studded lamps in their rooms.

VIII

"O Cloud! There will be other patches of
    clouds, ever-moving, like you,
They are carried up the seven-storied mansions,
They go into them moistening the paintings on
    the walls to ruin,
And as if seized with the fear of what they have
    done,
They escape at once out of windows and
    lattices,
Passing out as smoke, or as particles of water.

IX

"Where in a moonlit midnight water drops drip
From the network of threads hanging from the
    ceiling,
They fall on tired women released in languor
    from the embrace of their lovers.

X

"Where the rich spend their time with *Apsaras*
    in *Vaibhraja*,
The outer garden of the city,
While the *Kinnaras* sing of the glory of the *god*
    of riches.

XI

"Where the sunrise would show how lovelorn
    women traversed the path to their lovers late
    at night;
There will be *Mandara* flowers fallen from their
    braids,
And you will see broken petals of golden
    lotuses fallen from their ears.
And you will see pearls that have broken loose
    from necklaces on their expansive breasts.

XII

"They can get from the *wish-fulfilling tree*
All that a woman needs to decorate herself:
Garments of many colours,
Wine to intoxicate them to make them play
    gracefully with their eyes,
Fresh flowers with sprouts,
Ornaments of different kinds,
And dye to colour their tender lotus-like feet.

XIII

"Dark-green horses there,
Of the colour of the colour of leaves,
Do rival the sun's steeds;
Like you are the elephants high
And cast showers because of their ichor;
And their warriors bear scars,
Inflected by *Chandrahaas*, like ornaments.

XIV

"As *Shiva*, who is friendly to the *god of riches*,
Lives there too,
The *god of love* is afraid to use his bow
That has a row of bees for its string.
It is subtle women who carry out his intentions
    in a number of ways.
With lurid glances and playful brows,
They draw in those who are given to delicate
    lusts.

XV

"There, a little north of it, is my house,
That has a rainbow-like entrance gate to it.
And adjacent to it is a *wish-fulfilling tree*,
Nourished from the day it was planted by my
    wife.
One can pluck a bunch of its flowers from the
    ground.

XVI

"There is a tank close by,
With steps to it paved with emerald stones,
Full of blooming lotuses on glistening stalks.
The swans there are happy as they are,
Though you are there and *Manas* is close by.

XVII

"There is an artifice of a hill
Surrounded by a fence of golden plantain trees;
This is a sight for the eyes to see.
That hill is dear to my wife.
When I see you accompanied with lightning,
The sight saddens me, as alone and isolated,
I think of her for a moment on the hill without
    me.

XVIII

"There is a red *Ashoka* tree on it with
    simmering leaves
And a comely *Kesara* by its side,
Close to a bower of creeping *Madhavis*;
It is hedged in by *Kurbakas*.
That tree longs for a sudden contact, like me in
    the past,
With the left foot of your new friend;
And the latter gives mouthfuls of liquor to their
    roots to cause them to bloom.

XIX

"Between these two, there is a golden perch
That stands on a crystal slab.
It has its basement built with emeralds,
They look like fresh young green bamboos.
A peacock, as friendly as you are, resting on it
    in the evening before sunset, dances as she
    claps,
Her bracelets making a pleasant jingling sound.

XX

"You can surely discern
From the signs you remember,
Seeing *Shankha* and *Padma* painted on both
    sides of the door,
How sad my house looks without me.
You will find it is incapable like the lotus to
    retain its colour without the sun.

XXI

"You will first descend to that beautiful summit
Of that mount of pleasure,
Looking like a small elephant,
And cast your quick bright glance of lightning
Mildly like a glitter of fireworks.

XXII

"There you will find one quite young;
She is spare of build, with sharp pointed teeth
And lips red like a *Bimba* fruit;
Thin in the middle, with eyes as those of a doe
    surprised.
She has a deep navel, and a gait slow on
    account of the weight of her hips.
May be she stoops slightly because of her
    breasts;
You may take her to be the first of the Maker's
    creation of her own kind.

XXIII

"Know her to be reticent in speech and lovely,
Her companion being far away, like a
    Chakravaka, isolated from her mate.
I imagine she is changed in appearance,
While those heavy days press upon her
Like a lotus blighted by the cold wind.

XXIV

"I think she may have her face resting on her
    hand,
Eyes swollen on account of continued weeping;
With loose hair falling on that lovely face, it can
    only be seen in part.
Her lower lips dimmed due to the hot breaths
    she may be exhaling
And her face looking without lustre
    overshadowed by misery,
Like the moon trailing behind your movements.

XXV

"You may see her worship,
Or, painting me rendered lean by separation,
Or, she could be asking the sweet voiced *Sarika*
    in the cage,
'Sweet one, do you remember your master?
Was not he dear to you?'

XXVI

"O brother! You will see her in an unclean and
    faded wear,
Singing a song about me,
With the lute in her lap,
But the string wet with tears,
And the line slipping from her memory,
You may find her trying to set the strings again.

XXVII

"Or, she might be arranging flowers one by one
    on the threshold of her house,
Counting them and the remaining months of
    the period
From the day we separated,
Or the moments of our being together, shared
    enjoyment with me,
As conceived by the mind.
For this is how a woman comes to pass her time
    in separation from her consort.

XXVIII

"You may find she does not suffer so much in
    day time
For being kept away from me
As she must be busy with one work or another.
During night when she may be awake,
She may be thinking of me all the time.
You should, therefore, remain stationed at the
    window of the house,
And peep in at midnight,
To find out how that steadfast consort of mine
    is still awake.
She would be thinking of me as she lies half
    awake.
Tell her my message then.

XXIX

"Her friends would not leave that tender one
    alone in this condition,
For ladies do not like to desert their dear
    friends in such a state.
You should wait until her friends go to sleep,
    therefore;
Sit on the window of her room.

XXX

"And you will find her
Lying on one side of her body,
Pearls of her necklace lying scattered around,
Like drops of tear.
And she could be waiving aside time and again,
With her tapering nails,
The one loosely fashioned braid of her hair,
Which she would like to comb and set straight
    only after the curse ends.

XXXI

"Used to pass her night in complete enjoyment
    when we were together,
As if it were a brief stretch of time,
She must be weeping all the time now,
    shedding hot tears.
Wasted by anxiety due to separation,
She would look like the orb of the moon
    reduced to a single digit in the eastern skies.

XXXII

"She would think the moon rays coming
    through the windows
Are as cool now as when we were together,
But finding them hot and unbearable,
She would hide her eye-brows over the eyes full
    of tears.
My beloved may appear to you then like a half-
    open lotus on a cloudy day.

XXXIII

"She might be taking her bath these days with
plain cold water;
Her dry uncombed hair hence,
Hanging over her cheeks and thin lips
Would sometimes be shaken with the hot
    breaths
She exhales.

XXXIV

"You may find her swooning
Time and again due to her sorrows,
Falling sometimes unconscious to the floor.
You will find her without any outward show of
    beauty and ornaments,
Able to sustain herself with great difficulty.
Tears would come to your eyes then,
For what noble heart would not be affected by
    a painful situation.

XXXV

"When we were about to be separated—
She had unbraided her hair,
Tying it into a single knot,
For it pained her to touch it again.
But it fell loose all of a sudden,
Covering her full well-formed cheeks.
When the curse is ended,
I shall unfold that single knot of her braid
And tie it afresh happily once gain.

XXXVI

"I know your friend loves me intensely.
The sorrow, I suppose, of our first separation,
Might have rendered her lean.
Please do not think, I say this on account of her
    steadfast adherence to me, her consort.
You will find it yourself when you see it.

XXXVII

"When you arrive there,
The left eye of the doe-eyed one,
Unadorned, without kohl, will quiver.
And not used to employ them for quite
    sometime now,
She might have forgotten how to use her brows.
But you will find her quivering eyes still look
    beautiful,
Like a blue lotus when it is stirred about
    touched by the fishes in water.

XXXVIII

"Fair as a banana tree and as juicy,
Her left thigh would feel the quiver too.
I used to press it soothingly with my hand after
    our act of love.
You will not find any nail mark left on it,
Nor a pearl-string above it.

XXXIX

"O Cloud! If she is asleep as you arrive,
Wait there for sometime without thunder,
She might be in a deep embrace with me in her
    dream.
It would make her drop off her arms around my
    neck at once.

XL

"If she does not open her eyes after sleeping
    awhile,
Wake her, who is tender like blooming *Maltis*,
With a gentle thud of your sound;
Withhold the flash of your lightning, contained
    for some time.
Make the thunder speak a few words to her,
    that noble one.

XLI

"You will tell her, O fortunate one!
'I must tell you that a friend of your husband,
I have come to tell you a message:
That I do stir the heart of even wayfarers with
    the sound of thunder,
As they want to get back home to their wives,
And long to unravel the enmeshed single-
    braided fall of their hair.'

XLII

"Hearing this, she would turn to you and listen
    carefully
With an open heart whatever you have to say,
Like *Sita* who listened to the *Son of the Wind.*
For O gentle one!
To women tidings about their consorts are as
    good as actual union.

XLIII

"O you, of the long life! Tell her
As you have been good to me
And want to be good to others,
'O helpless one! Your husband is safe at
    Ramagiri Ashrama
And wants to know how you fare,'
You should say this to her,
As this is the right thing to tell her, as
She has fallen upon bad days.

XLIV

"Tell her that fate itself obstructs the path of
    her dear one:
He may not be able to meet her,
But looking at his own condition,
Emaciated, afflicted with tension all the time,
    breathing heavily,
He does understand you too —
'How separation has made you lean, and how
    you might be pining,
Shedding tears, eager to meet and exhaling
    warm sighs.

XLV

'"One, who would feign whisper into your ears,
Something that could be said aloud before your
	friends,
Only to be able to touch your face,
Sends you this message, which must be heard
	alone,
Words arranged under the inspiration of what
	he longs for.

XLVI

"'I see your physique in a graceful creeper,
Your sight in the gaze of a doe overtaken by
	surprise,
Your face in how the bright moon looks,
Your well-combed hair in the plumage of a
	peacock,
And the gentle ripple in your eyes in the
	simmering of a river.
But Oh dear! Thou art a vital one.
None of them do measure up to your
	attractions.

XLVII

"'When I draw your image in anger on a stone
    slab in orange-yellow mineral dyes,
Myself lying prostrate at your feet,
To placate you,
My tears obscure my eyes,
I cannot see.
Fate is still adverse;
It would not allow us to a union even so.

XLVIII

"'My Lady, I must say the sap in me dries up far
    from that mouth of yours;
It smells of the earth after a light drizzle.
And the *god of love* is as unsparing,
He keeps on shooting his five arrows.
It is for you to think if I shall be able to spend
    my days here,
For thick clouds will cover the sun soon.

XLIX

"'As I try to catch you passing through many an
    obstruction in a tight embrace,
Arising out of my vision in dreams,
Deities of the place shed tears as big as pearls
    from above.

L

"'I embrace the breeze from the snowy
    mountain above,
That passes through the deodars,
Breaking their tender new leaves, laden with the
    smell of fresh sap, O virtuous one!
Thinking they bear your touches.

LI

"'With your tremulous eyes in mind,
I always desire that the long period
Of the *three-quartered stretch* of
Our sleeping time should contract itself into a
    brief hour.
But my prayer is wasted,
And add to it the depressing pangs of our
    separation.

LII

"'I have been able to sustain myself with deep
    reflection, O blessed one!
You should not remain, therefore, unhappy either
For joys and sorrows do always alternate.

LIII

"'When *Vishnu*, holder of the horny bow,
Would rise from the *Serpent-bed*,
My curse will come to an end.
Spend, therefore, the remaining four months
    with closed eyes.
We will meet then in the moonlit winter night
Fulfilling all such desires
That lay dormant within our hearts.

LIV

"'And your dear husband told me again,
How when you were sleeping once
With his arms around his neck,
You woke up suddenly.
And when he asked you the reason for it,
You said smiling,
'You rogue, I saw you having a good time with
    another woman in dream.'

LV

"O dark-eyed Lady! You should take it to be a
 proof
That I am well:
And you should not doubt my love because of
 hearsay.
I do not know why people say
Love is lessened in separation.
The desire for it, on the contrary,
Is heightened, accumulating into heaps of love.'

LVI

"You should consider your friend, who suffers,
Because this is our first separation.
You should come back
From that mountain whose peaks have been
 dug up by *Shiva's bull.*
And pray for me too;
The delicate thread of whose life is brittle.
It hangs loosely like flowering *Kundas* of the
 morning that can fall at the slightest touch.

LVII

"Do you agree to do it for me, O gentle one!
Seeing you grave, I infer
You do affirm my supplication.
I do not want a reply from you,
Or take your grave silence to be rejection either.
You do give the *Chatakas* rare drops of water to
    drink without asking for it.
The benign ones do not so much like to talk
    about a deed as to accomplish what is
    expected of them.

LVIII

"Having done this for me,
Though I am not worthy of it,
Out of compassion for me,
For what I have suffered in separation,
O Cloud! Wander over what you will in
    splendour
That the rains bring to you.
May you not ever suffer separation from your
    better half,
Even for a moment.

Notes on *The Meghaduta*

There is a clear structural design in the poem based on a journey from Ramagiri to the whereabouts of Mount Kailasha in the North-West. An exercise in fantasy, the journey to Alakapuri corresponds to actual details of the landscape which remains the same today as in the past, but for the change of some of the names due to linguistic transformations. That one can refer these place names back to their origins evinces the poet's sure grasp of his environment in creating an authentic poem. Thus, Ramagiri becomes Ramtek, Ujjaini Ujjain, Vetrawati Betwa, Amrakuta Amarkantak, Dewagiri Devgarh, Charmawati Chambal, Manas Sarovar Manasarovar, and Vindhyapad Vindhya.

Some of the names remain the same, denoting marvellous continuity in perception which becomes a source of the poet's realism, as in the use of place names or the names of rivers or mountains such as Kankhal or Shipra (also Kshipra) or Kailasha. This he draws upon in combination with his great talent for mythopoeia. (The genesis of myths handled by Kalidasa deserves to be studied in depth on their own.) Both the aspects of the poem have been fused into one as they have been integrated into a unity of apprehension coming of a complex mood based on the evocation of a dominant emotion. The poem, hence, has been read as a remarkable expression of youthful love in world literature.

Fusion of the details of landscape as it can be perceived in a journey in the rainy season with the historical and cultural

67

past or pasts of the areas the cloud passes through, is based on the poet's own experiences of them. So the poem reads like a slow-motion film. Coming after the two greatest epic poets in Sanskrit as they have been able to project the possibility of a great Indian tradition in literature and life, Kalidasa goes ahead in his power to absorb this tradition and take it further ahead in poetry. He comes to have new innovations in his power to understand the past in his time in strikingly new ways in so far as he can re-integrate his own experiences with those of his people on a universal basis deriving from the ideas, beliefs and myths from the Vedas, the Upanishads and the epics before him. It is in this sense, he emerges as one of the supreme poets of the Indian culture and civilisation at its best even in a love poem such as *The Meghduta*. The notes below draw heavily on free online material including Wikipedia and hence, are out of the purview of the author's copyright.

Agni: Literally, the word means fire. It is the name of the Hindu god of fire, one of the most significant gods of Hinduism from the Vedic to present times. No Hindu religious ceremony is complete without him. He is the symbol of purity; of life as the fire of the sun. He accepts of offerings on behalf of all gods, and as jatharagni (fire of stomach) consumes food and sustains life. Agni is said to be the son of ten mothers symbolising the ten fingers on the human hand. He is depicted with two faces suggesting his destructive and beneficent qualities; seven tongues, wild black hair, two hands and three legs. He rides a ram or a chariot. Agni loves all his worshipers equally, and so is loved in turn by all of them. He visits everyone's hearth, rich or poor. Usha (dawn) and Nisha (night) are his sisters and the sacrificial chant, Svaha is his wife. Pavaka (electric fire, lightening), Pavamana (produced by friction), and Suchi (solar or celestial fire) are his three sons. The *Rigveda* begins with a reference to Agni and as many as 218 out of 1,028 hymns are addressed to him. Eight of its ten books begin with praises dedicated to Agni. (Purva Meghah XLVII)

Airavata: Is the name of the elephant of Indra, the king of gods. He is described in mythological texts as white in colour with three heads, four tusks and seven trunks. Indra rides Airavata to war. The elephant also sucks water in his trunk and sprays it into the clouds which Indra uses to make rain. Even today, when there is drought people in India pray to Indra for rain. According to one version of his origin, Airavata and Indra's horse Ucchaisravas came out of Samudra Manthan (churning of the ocean). Airavata stands guard at the entrance of Indra's palace. (Purva Meghah LXVI)

Alaka: Inhabited by the Yakshas and ruled by Kubera, it is a mythical city in the north-western Himalayas. In this poem, Kalidasa makes use of the existence of such a city as per an available classical myth to a poetic advantage in a tale of his own making. (Purva Meghah VII, LXVII)

Amrakuta: Also known as Amarkantak, it is a hill station and pilgrimage spot situated at an altitude of 1,065 metres in Anuppur district of Madhya Pradesh state in central India. This is where the Vindhya and the Satpura mountain ranges meet. The Maikal Hills form the fulcrum of their meeting. This is also where the Narmada and Sone rivers emerge from moist Sal and mixed forests. While the Narmada flows westwards, the Sone (also called Sonbhadra because of its placid flow and golden sand) flows towards the east. Narmada, believed to be over 150 million years older than the Ganga, is considered by a section of Hindus even more sacred than the latter. It is said that once every year, the Ganga, polluted herself by washing the sins of people, assumes the form of a woman and comes to take a dip in the Narmada to purify herself. Amarkantak is also believed to be the place where one attains Nirvana, or Mukti or salvation. There are a number of beautiful waterfalls around Amarkantak including the one at the junction of Anuppur and Dindori districts where the Narmada drops over 20 metres down a sheer basalt rock. These hills are also home to some of the most primitive tribes of Madhya Pradesh like the Hill Korwas and Pandavas. (Purva Meghah XVII, XIX)

Apsara: Is a female mythological angelic creature akin to celestial maidens or nymphs. They are described as extremely beautiful and accomplished in the art of dancing. They are endowed with eternal youth. They dance to the music played by the Gandharvas to entertain the gods and their guests. There were said to be 26 principal Apsaras at Indra's court, each representing a distinct aspect of the performing arts, and in that sense, they are like the muses of Greek mythology. When gods felt threatened by persons practising rigid austerities they employed Apsaras to break their penance. The concept is also present in several other Asian cultures influenced by Hinduism and Buddhism. (Uttara Meghah X)

Arjuna: Is the name of the third of the five Pandava brothers. He was said to have been born of Indra, the king of gods. As the only warrior in the epic *Mahabharata* who did not suffer defeat till the end, he is considered the hero of the story. Portrayed as the achiever, he is imbued with the qualities of perseverance, singularity of purpose and clarity of mind. The only time he is confused is when the war is about to start. That is when Krishna his charioteer, guides him through his discourse that is *Bhagavad-Gita*. The word Arjuna means shining white, spotless and clean of all impurities and hence, a fit receptacle of divine wisdom and the highest knowledge. In the *Rigveda*, the clear, sunny and bright day is referred to as 'Arjunam.' (Purva Meghah LII)

Asadha: Is the fourth month of the Indian calendar and corresponds to the June-July period. This is the period of the advent of the south-west summer monsoon. (Purva Meghah II)

Ashoka (*Saraca Indica/Asoca*): Is a small, erect evergreen rain-forest tree with deep green leaves borne in dense clusters. It grows all over India barring the high mountains. The young wavy leaves are soft and red in colour. From February to April it bears bright orange-yellow flowers in heavy, lush bunches that turn red before wilting. Perhaps that is why the Yaksha talks of a red Ashoka at his home. The beautiful tree is found in wild and also grown in gardens. With a host of religious associations for Hindus, Buddhists and Jains, the tree is often grown around temples. It finds wide mention in Sanskrit literature including the Puranans and the epics. The tree's bark, seed and flowers have medicinal properties which could have been a factor in it being called *ashoka* which means "without sorrow". Extracts are used in treatment of several ailments of women. (Uttara Meghah XVIII)

Avanti: It was one of the *mahajanpadas* (great country) of ancient India. Located in west central India, it was divided into north and south provinces by river Vetrawati (Betwa). Avanti occupied the Malwa region where the present state of Madhya Pradesh is located. It was an important Buddhist centre and later became a part of Magadha Empire. The *mahajanpadas* started off as small settlements, also referred to as republics, but expanded to become bigger monarchical entities and 16 of them are mentioned in the ancient literature and scriptures as the greatest of them all. Avanti was one of the four most important *mahajanpadas*. (Purva Meghah XXXII)

Balarama: The elder brother of Vishnu's incarnation Krishna, Balarama was the son of Vasudeva and Rohini, and is considered an incarnation of Shesha, the king of serpents who forms the bed of Vishnu. On account of his immense strength, he is called Baladeva. On account of being simple and straightforward (unlike Krishna who was not averse to using guile), he is called Balabhadra. As he carries hala (plough) as his ayudha (arm), he is called Halayudha. As a role model who attracts the Yadavas to follow in his path, he is Sankarshana. He taught both Bhima, the second Pandava brother, and his eldest Kaurava cousin Duryodhana, the art of fighting with the mace. In the Mahabharata war he remained neutral, but when Bhima killed Duryodhana by hitting him below the waist with his mace, Balarama threatened to kill Bhima. However, Kirshna reminded him that Bhima had vowed to kill Duryodhana by breaking the thigh he had exposed to the Pandava brothers' wife Draupadi saving the day for Bhima. Balarama married Rewati and had two sons both of whom died in the fratricidal Yadava war that followed from a curse. After their death, Balarama sat in meditation by the sea and put and end to the incarnation. (Purva Meghah LIII)

Bali: Was a benevolent and generous king of the Asura (demonic) race in the line of Hiranyakashipu and was the grandson of Prahlada who had taken over the heavens from Indra. Vishnu incarnated as Vamana (midget) to restore it to Indra. Disguised as a Brahmana he asked for alms of three paces of land. Despite his guru Shukracharya warning against it, Bali granted the request. Then Vamana grew into a giant and covered heaven, earth and the netherworld (Patalaloka) in two steps. Bali offered his head for Vamana to place his third step. Vamana then placed his foot on his head and pushed him out of the earth. (Purva Meghah LXI)

Bhavani: Means giver of life and is a name of Parvati, the consort of Shiva. The power of nature or the source of creative energy, she is known as Karunaswaroopini (epitome of mercy), but she also has a ferocious aspect. In the latter aspect, she is seen as having eight arms holding various weapons and the head of the demon Mahishasura (buffalo demon). According to legends, the Mother Goddess Shakti assumed this form after absorbing the powers of the other mothers including Varaahi, Bhrahmi, Vaishnavi, Kaumaari, Indraani and Saambhavi when the gods, terrorised by the demon Matanga approached her for help on the advice of Bhrahma. (Purva Meghah XLVIII)

Bimba (*Coccinia indica*): Also known as Kundru or Kundri, Bimba is the fruit of a tropical creeper that grows in the wild in Asia and Africa and is extensively eaten as a vegetable in India. Known as ivy gourd in English, the fruit is green when unripe and turns scarlet on ripening. That is why the Yaksha has compared his wife's lips to the fruit. The plant has been used in traditional medicine as a household remedy for various diseases, including fever, asthma, bronchitis, jaundice, biliary disorders, anorexia, diabetes, as well as hepatic disorders. It has been shown to have anti-inflammatory, antioxidant, anti-diabetic, antibacterial, anti-protozoal, anti-ulcer, expectorant, analgesic and anti-inflammatory properties. (Uttara Meghah XXII)

Brahmavarta: The word means the land of gods. According to *Manusmriti*, it was the land between the now extinct rivers Saraswati and the Drisadwati. There is much debate and little certainty among scholars about the location of the two rivers and consequently Brahmavarta. It is also said that the place which first witnessed the creation of mankind came to be known as Brahmavarta or the seat of Brahma. In the town of Bithoor situated on the bank of the Ganga in Kanpur district of Uttar Pradesh state of India there is a place called Brahmavarta Ghat where the Shivalinga is worshipped as Brahmeshwar Mahadeva. (Purva Meghah LII)

Chakravaka: Also known as Chakva, it is identified with Ruddy Shelduck (*Tadorna ferruginea*) also called Brahmani Duck. It is a member of the swan or goose family. It has orange-brown body plumage and a paler head. The wings are white with black flight feathers. It swims well, and in flight looks heavy, more like a goose than a duck. The male and female are similar, but the male has a black ring at the bottom of the neck in summer, the breeding season. The female often has a white face patch. They are mostly migratory, wintering in the Indian subcontinent. The main breeding area is from south east Europe across central Asia to South-east Asia though they are found in small numbers in western Africa and Ethiopia. In Hindu art and poetry, it represents constancy and conjugal affection like in the stories of Nala-Damayanti and Dushyanta-Shakuntala. According to legends, the Chakravakas were cursed by Rama for ridiculing his loneliness when he was wandering in the forests, looking for Sita after Ravana had kidnapped her. That is why they fly in pairs during the day and separate during night calling one another piteously through the night. The dialogue is said to be "Chakava, may I come to you?"; "No, Chakavi." The species is usually found dispersed in pairs during the breeding season, although it may form small nesting groups when desirable nesting sites are close together. They are depicted in the Buddhist Wheel of Life called Bhavachakra where they symbolise obsessive lust which can never be satiated except through enlightenment of Nirvana or salvation. (Uttara Meghah XXIII)

Chandrahaas: Is the name of the sword given by Shiva to Ravana. The literal meaning of the word is 'the laughter of the moon' and it refers to the crescent shape of the sword. When Ravana went to meet Shiva at his abode in Kailasha Nandi the bull and Shiva's vehicle, refused to let Ravana in. An angry Ravana began shaking the Kailasha in a bid to uproot it disturbing a meditating Shiva in the process. The god, in order to teach the arrogant demon king a lesson, pinned him under the mountain with his little toe causing him to cry out in pain (the terrible cry earned him the name Ravana). Realising his mistake, Ravana composed and sung songs in praise of Shiva for years, until finally a pleased Shiva not only released him but also gave him the Chandrahaas. He, however, also warned Ravana that if the sword was used for an unjust cause, it would return to Shiva and would signal the approach of Ravana's end. The sword returned to Shiva after Ravana used it to kill Jatayu when the wise vulture, a devotee of Rama, tried to foil his bid to kidnap Sita. When Kalidasa refers of the Yaksha warriors wearing as ornaments the scars of wounds inflicted by Chandrahaas, he is perhaps, talking about the conflict that might have taken place between the armies of Ravana and Kubera over Lanka though it must have been a very limited engagement as Kubera was no match for Ravana. In fact, Alaka was created to compensate Kubera for the loss of Lanka. (Uttara Meghah XIII)

Charmawati: Also Charmanyawati and Charmanwati was the ancient name of the river now called Chambal. It is a perennial river and a tributary of the Yamuna. It originates in the Vindhyas near Mhow in Indore district of Madhya Pradesh state, flows through Rajasthan and then through Uttar Pradesh before joining the Yamuna River in Etawah district in the same state. Shipra, Choti Kalisindh, Sivanna, Retam, Ansar, Kalisindh, Banas, Parbati, Seep, Kuwari, Kuno, Alnia, Mej, Chakan, Parwati, Chamla, Gambhir, Lakhunder, Khan, Bangeri, Kedel and Teelar are its tributaries. The name Chambal in some Indian languages means fish, thus linking the river to the fish (Matsya in Sanskrit) tribe. It is argued that as this community grew in power, it attained kingship and gave rise to the Matsya kingdom. The river, according to the *Mahabharata*, formed the southern boundary of Panchala kingdom and when the unmarried Kunti gave birth to Karna and put the new-born baby in a basket to float on the Aswa River (a tributary), the basket drifted on the water to Charmanwati, Yamuna and Ganga eventually reaching Champapuri the capital of Anga country. The story of its origin is rather unusual. According to it, secretions flowing from the charma (hide) of countless animals (including cows) sacrificed by king Rantideva everyday for feeding his guests took the form of a river. That is where it got its name from. The story is mentioned in the *Mahabharata* and often held as proof of cow slaughter in ancient India. But the *Mahabharata* also says that at a later date cows were no longer considered animals fit for sacrifice. They were instead considered animals fit for gift. (Purva Meghah XLIX, LI)

Chataka: Identified with Papiha (*Clamator jacobinus*), Chataka is a bird that is said (in Indian literature) to wait for the first rain of the Swati *nakshatra* (one of the 27 sub-divisions of 13 degrees and 20 minutes of the zodiac, and named after the most prominent group of stars in that sector) to drink water. That is the only time it drinks. During its long wait, it keeps looking at the sky and is also said to be very fond of the moon. The bird signifies a lover's yearning as well as patience. It is commonly referred to as pied crested cuckoo. Wikipedia quotes Satya Churn Law, saying that in Bengal, the bird associated with the 'chataka' was the common Iora (*Aegithina tiphia*). (Purva Meghah X, XXIII, Uttara Meghah LVII)

Counterfeit of Vishnu: Kalidasa compares the dark reflection of the cloud in the water to the dark colour of Vishnu. (Purva Meghah L)

Dasharna: It is the ancient name of the river now known as Dhasana, a tributary of Betwa. In *Mahabharata* there is mention of two Dasharna kingdoms, one in the part of Punjab, which is now in Pakistan and the other, in north-eastern parts of Madhya Pradesh. Here, Kalidasa seems to be talking of the latter located as it is in the eastern Malwa region with Vidisha as its capital. The region was inhabited by Dasharna, Dasharh, Kuntal and Charman tribes. Dashpur, which means the abode of or the city of Dashas seems to refer to the capital of Dasharna kingdom. (Purva Meghah XXV)

Dashpur: See Dasharna (Purva Meghah LI)

Dewagiri: It has been placed by Kalidasa between Ujjain and Mandasaur near Chambal. It is identified by scholars with Devgarh situated in the centre of the province of Malwa on the southern bank of the Chambal. (Purva Meghah XLVI)

Footprints of Rama on his slopes: See Ramagiri (Purva Meghah XII).

Gambhira: Is a tributary of the Shipra in Malwa. (Purva Meghah XLIV)

Ganas: Are the attendants of Shiva and Ganesha or Ganapti (the king of the ganas) is their leader. (Purva Meghah LIX)

Gandharva: In Indian mythology the Gandharvas are generally handsome male creatures with human as well as non-human characteristics. Well versed in music, art and medicine to the extent of appearing to have magical charms and the power to create illusions, they sang for the gods and were in charge of Soma, the intoxicating liquor drunk by the gods. Their female counterparts often called their wives or mates were the dancers of the gods, the Apsaras. In the *Mahabharata*, apparently, a race of people dwelling in the hills and wilds is referred to as Gandharva. Chitraratha was chief of the Gandharvas. The cities of the Gandharvas are often referred to as being very splendid. The *Atharvaveda* speaks of the 6,333 Gandharvas. (Purva Meghah L)

Gandhawati: It is a small branch of the Shipra on which the temple of Mahakala is situated. (Purva Meghah XXXVII)

Gandiva: It was the name of the bow used by Arjuna, the hero of the epic *Mahabharata*. Said to be created by Brahma, it passed through the hands of the Prajapati, Indra, Soma and Varuna before coming to Arjuna along with his Hanuman-bannered chariot, and two inexhaustible quivers. The radiant-ended bow was worshiped by Devas, Gandharvas and Danavas or demons. It is said that besides Krishna no mortal but Arjuna could wield the bow which produced a twang that was like thunder. After the Mahabharata war, Arjuna had to return the Gandiva along with the quivers to Varuna. (Purva Meghah LII)

Ganga: It is the most sacred river for Hindus and is worshiped like the mother. Her water is kept in Hindu households and used in all religious functions for purification. A dip in the Ganga is said to absolve one of all sins. Bathing in the river at Gangotri, Haridwar, Prayaga and Varanasi are considered especially significant. According to traditional Hindu beliefs, invoking the Ganga, which has descended from heaven, lends any water the attributes of the holy river. There is a tradition of consigning the ashes of a person after cremation to the Ganga.

This brings salvation to the soul of the dead as the river that comes from the heaven and goes to the netherworld passing the earth (Triloka-patha-gamini) is also the one that shows the path to it. Death at Varanasi, the Mahashmashana or the Great Cremation Ground, and cremation on the banks of the Ganga, bring instant salvation. Hindus also perform on the banks of the Ganga Pindadana, a rite for the dead, which is supposed to bring salvation for ancestors who might have fallen from heaven after their term there, earned on account their good deeds, ends. The river originates in the western Himalayas in Uttarakhand state of India and falls into the Bay of Bengal in Bangladesh. It is India's longest river and the second greatest river in the world by water discharge. Its banks have seen in course of history the rise and fall of important cities, states, kingdoms and empires like Pataliputra, Kannauj, Kara, Kashi, Allahabad, Murshidabad, Munger, Baharampur, Kampilya and Kolkata. The descent of the Ganga to earth is celebrated as Ganga Dashahra. It falls on the tenth day of the waxing moon of the third month in the Hindu calendar Jyestha (May-June). While some versions of the river's *avartana* (descent) to earth credit it to Indra or Vishnu, the most widely told legend credits it to Bhagiratha. According to the story, once Vishnu in the form of the sage Kapila was meditating when the sixty thousand sons of king Sagara looking for the sacrificial horse of their father stolen by a demoness found it near the sage, and taking him to be the culprit, attacked him. Disturbed out of his meditation, the angry Kapila burnt them down to ashes with one fiery gaze. Only the waters of the Ganga, then flowing in heaven, could bring them salvation. Later, after Anshumat, his grandson from another son, helped bring to conclusion king Sagara's *yagna* (holy rituals), he tried his best to bring down the mighty Ganga for the salvation of his uncles but failed. So did his son Dilipa. After generations of fruitless effort his son Bhagiratha by dint of his rigorous penance got from Brahma the boon of Ganga's descent from heaven. To avoid the catastrophic results of the river's fall on earth Shiva, pleased by Bhagirath's worship, agreed to receive her in the coils of his matted hair. As a haughty Ganga fell Shiva let her wander in his locks and Bhagiratha had to do many austerities again before Shiva let the by-now-fully-tamed Ganga find her way to earth. From there she arrived in the Himalayas and was led by the waiting Bhagiratha down. On way, she flooded the hermitage of Jahnu who got angry and drank up all her waters to release from his ear only after the intervention of numerous gods and sages. Thus, flowing behind Bhagiratha, she crossed Haridwar and Prayaga and Varanasi and finally reached Ganga Sagar, where on meeting the ocean, she sank to the netherworld and brought salvation to the sons of Sagara. That is why Ganga is also called Bhagirathi. (Purva Meghah XLVII, LXVII)

Gauri: It is another name of Parvati. It means the fair one and is used for the consort of Shiva because of her complexion. Gauri is considered the Kanya (young, unmarried) Parvati who having undergone severe penance in order to get Lord Shiva as her husband also represents purity and austerity. Unmarried Hindu girls worship Gauri to get a virtuous and loving husband like Shiva. Even Sita, the consort of Rama, had worshipped Gauri to fulfil her desire to marry Rama. Talking about the white foam of Ganga as making fun of Gauri, Kalidasa imbues Ganga with the qualities of a playful young maiden who evokes distrust in Gauri as she descends from the heavens into the dreadlocks of Shiva. (Purva Meghah LIV, LXIV)

God of love: See Kamadeva (Uttara Meghah XIV, XLVIII)

God of riches: It refers to Kubera, the king of Yakshas and other divine beings, who is the treasurer of gods, and finds place in the Hindu, Buddhist as well as Jain pantheons. Guardian of North, keeper of treasures of the earth, bestower of prosperity, he was ruler of the fabled city state of Lanka till his half-brother Ravana usurped his kingdom as well as his flying craft Pushpaka. Since Lanka which rightfully belonged to him could not be restored to him on account of Ravana being invincible at that point of time, Vishwakarma, the architect of the gods, built for him the city of Alakapuri in the Himalayas close to Kailasha, the abode of Shiva whose devotee both Kubera and Ravana were. He is also said to have a beautiful garden on Mount Mandara. He is depicted as a dwarfish figure with a white body, three legs and eight teeth. His body is covered with jewels and ornaments. He has two or four hands and may carry in his hand a mace, a purse containing money, a vase, a fruit and a bowl or have two hands in the boon giving and protective modes. If shown as having two hands he carries a bowl and a money-bag. (Uttara Meghah X, XIV)

Himvanta: It is another name for the Himalaya which means one who has snow. (Purva Meghah LIX)

Jahnu's daughter or Jahanvi: It is another name of the river Ganga. See Ganga (Purva Meghah LIV)

Jamun (*Syzygium cumini*): Also called Jambul, it is a fast growing tall evergreen tropical tree found all over India. According to Hindu tradition, Rama used to eat the fruit during his fourteen years of vanvasa (living in forests) in exile from Ayodhya. The fruits are a good source of iron and are said to be useful in the troubles of heart and liver. The seed and bark have several applications in traditional systems of medicine. The seeds have anti-diabetic properties and their powder is used to control diabetes. They are also used as antidote in soft-food poisoning and as cattle feed. The bark has tonic and astringent properties. It is generally grown as an avenue tree or as wind break. The fairly hard and reasonably durable, though not so easily workable, wood is used in cheap village dwellings, agricultural implements, cheap furniture, etc. (Purva Meghah XXV)

Janaki: Means the daughter of Janaka and is another name of Sita, the consort of the Rama. As per Hindu mythology Sita was an incarnation of Lakshmi, goddess of wealth and wife of Vishnu while Rama himself was the incarnation of the latter. The poet is referring to her ablutions during the time when she, her husband Rama and brother-in-law Lakshmana stayed there during Rama's fourteen-year exile from Ayodhya. (Purva Meghah I)

Kadamba (*Anthocephalus indicus*): It is a deciduous tree which grows throughout India, especially at low levels and in wet places. It has a straight stem about twenty meres tall and up to two metres in girth with drooping branches and big leaves. The bark is dark grey in colour, exfoliating in thin scales. Flowers are sweetly fragrant, red to orange in colour, occurring in dense, globular heads. The green-brown colour of the flower mentioned by Kalidasa appears to be referring to the buds that are just opening. It is one of the most useful herbs mentioned in all ancient Sanskrit scriptures and *Ayurvedic* texts with bark, leaves, fruits, roots all having great medicinal value. It is said to be useful in curing diabetes, skin diseases, urinary ailments, wounds, ulcer, diarrhoea, dysentery, colitis, cough, fever, vomiting, inflammation of eyes and even snake-bites. It is also said to be of use as astringent, birth control agent and for enhancing breast milk in lactating mothers. A yellow dye is obtained from the root bark and the flowers are used in the production of *attar*, a type of perfume. In north India, it is associated with Krishna and in the south it is known as Parvati's tree. (Purva Meghah XXII, XXVII)

Kalpa tree: Also known as Kalpavriksha or Kalpataru, it is said in Indian mythology to be a tree in Heaven that grants fulfilment of desires. Along with Kamdhenu, the cow that fulfils all wishes, it is said to have been discovered during Samudra Manthan or churning of the ocean. At Jyotirmath, Badrinath in Uttaranchal, renowned as the residence of Adiguru Shankaracharya, there is a large, ancient mulberry tree known locally as the Kalpavriksha. Sometimes the banyan tree is also referred to as Kalpavriksha. There are several other trees at specific places referred to as Kalpavriksha. In some coastal areas, the coconut tree is referred to as Kalpavriksha or Kalpataru because of its ability to amply provide for human needs. (Purva Meghah LXVI)

Kamadeva: Also known simply as Kama, he is the god of desire (or human love) in the Hindu pantheon, akin to Cupid or Eros. The word *kama* means desire. He is some places considered the son of Brahma as desire or wish has been told to be the first movement that arose in Him. In earlier texts he is the deity credited for the wish of general well-being or common good. His influence is considered a positive mover in worldly affairs, from creation to invention, through effort. His names like Kandarpa (inflamer even of a god), Manmatha (churner of hearts) and Madana (delightful) indicate the impact various types of wishes can have on humans and even gods. According to Hindu mythology, once when the gods were greatly distressed by the demon named Taraka, looking for a remedy to the situation, they found that only a son of Shiva could destroy the demon. The problem was that due to his intense grief at the loss of his wife Sati, Shiva had become insensitive to the desire. So Indra, the king of gods, sought the help of Kamadeva. He succeeded in his effort and Shiva fell in love with Parvati (Sati reborn) but not before his anger at the interruption in his meditation had reduced Kama to ashes. Then Rati, Kamadeva's consort, the goddess of beauty, pleaded to Parvati to ask Shiva to restore her husband's life. So Kamadeva was born as Pradyumna (he who conquers all), the son of Krishna (Vishnu's incarnation) and Rukmini (Lakshmi's incarnation) to be tended and brought up by Mayadevi (Rati) and that is how he is said to be an image of Vishnu. The tale alludes to the importance of desire in keeping the world going. Kama is usually represented as a beautiful youth, holding in his hands a bow and arrows of flowers. He travels the Heaven, Earth and the Netherworld, his sugarcane bow in hand, and accompanied wife Rati, the cuckoo, the humming-bee, Vasanta (spring), gentle breezes and the parrot. He is worshipped at the time of marriage, and marital happiness and offspring, are sought from him. His arrows are decorated with the flowers of Ashoka tree, white and blue lotuses, Mallika tree (Jasmine) and mango tree. The Holi festival, which is celebrated in spring, is also called Madana-Mahotsava in Sanskrit. (Uttara Meghah IV)

Kandali (*Strobilanthes wallichii*): Also known as Jyotilaa or Bichhoo Ghas, Kashmir Acanthus, Hardy Persian Shield, and Wild Petunia is a herbaceous perennial, native to the Himalayas that bears pale blue flowers when it blooms once every twelve years, an occasion which is celebrated with the Kandali Festival in the Pithoragarh district of Uttaranchal state of India. The bloom season stays for five to six months. The leaves are cooked and eaten in Uttaranchal as a green leafy vegetable dish after hard boiling to ensure acidity of the leaves is removed. (Purva Meghah XXII)

Kankhal: Is the name of a religious spot on the foothills of the Himalayas mentioned in the *Mahabharata* and other religious texts which is now part of Haridwar town in Uttaranchal state of India. For long it was a much larger town than Haridwar as wealthy Hindus built homes there. Taking a dip in the Ganga here is said to wash away one's sins. It one of the five mandated pilgrim spots within Haridwar. The Daksha Mahadeva temple is located here. It is said that Shiva agreed to stay here perpetually in the form of a lingam on the request of king Daksha the father of his wife Sati who initially would not accept the god as son-in-law. Daksha's obduracy led to the self immolation of his daughter and hugely enraged Shiva. Vishnu had to intervene to cool down Shiva. Even Daksha later became a devotee of Shiva as per the tale related to the Kankhal's Daksha Mahadeva temple. (Purva Meghah LIV)

Kesara (Crocus sativussativus): Better known by its English name saffron, Kesara is a small herb upto twenty-five centimetres in height which bears light violet, reddish-purple or mauve coloured flowers. It has five to eleven white and non-photosynthetic leaves that cover and protect as many thin, straight, and blade-like true green foliage leaves as they bud and develop after the flowers have opened, or simultaneously with them. One plant bears up to four flowers, each with three vivid crimson stigmas. The contrasting colours of the long leaves and the big flower present a visually striking image that Kalidasa is referring to while drawing a word-picture of the Yaksha's home. The mention of a single plant sharpens the image. The spice derived from the flower (stalks that connect the stigmas to their host plant and the dried stigmas) are used mainly in various cuisines as a seasoning and colouring agent. Saffron also contains more than 150 volatile and aroma-yielding compounds. The perennial plant is unknown in the wild and originated possibly when the eastern Mediterranean autumn-flowering *Crocus cartwrightianus* also known as "wild saffron" was subjected to extensive artificial selection by growers seeking longer stigmas. The documented history of saffron cultivation spans more than three millennia. First believed to have been cultivated in Greece, saffron, the most expensive spice in the world, is now produced in several countries but Iran alone accounts for 90 percent of the global production. Over thousands of years saffron has been used in the treatment of many illnesses. Alexander the Great used Persian saffron in his infusions, rice, and baths as a curative for battle wounds. Saffron is believed to have come to Kashmir in India (close to Yaksha's house in mythical Alakapuri) around 500 BC but that is where the best saffron still comes from. (Uttara Meghah XVIII)

Ketaki (*Pandanus odoratissimus/ Pandanus tectorius* and *fascicularis*): Also known as Kewda, in English it is called the fragrant screwpine, umbrella tree or caldera bush. Other Indian names include Gagan-dhul, Tikshna-gandha and Sugandhini. It is a shrub or a small tree, with many aerial roots, narrow leaves up to 150 cm long, very fragrant flowers that bloom in summer and large pineapple-like fruits. It grows all over India but is found wild in south India, Andamans and Myanmar. Male flowers are used to obtain aromatic oil (Kewda attar) and fragrant Kewda water used to flavour food. The powerful perfume is effective even after drying. The tender leaves are eaten raw or cooked with condiments. All parts of the plant are of medicinal value. Interestingly, Hindus consider it as a flower cursed by Shiva for bearing a false witness of Lord Brahma and do not offer it while performing puja or worship. (Purva Meghah XXV)

Kinnara: They are semi-divine beings like the Yakshas and Gandharvas. Known for their exotic beauty and eternal youth, they are depicted as living a life of perpetual pleasure on the Himvanta (Himalayas). They are also renowned for their artistic accomplishments and skills like singing and dancing. They are also seen as a tribe mentioned along with Devas (including Rudras, Maruts, Vasus and Adityas), Asuras (including Daityas, Danavas and Kalakeyas), Pisachas, Gandharvas, Kimpurushas, Vanaras, Suparnas, Rakshasas, Bhutas and Yakshas. They, along with the others, were inhabitants of the Mandara Mountains in the Himalayas. According to a legend, Kinnaras were the troops of Ila, the king who was transformed into a woman due to a curse and became the wife of Buddha (planet Mercury). In *Mahabharata* Kinnaras are described as half-man, half-horse creatures. (Purva Meghah LX, Uttara Meghah X)

Krishna: Is the name of a Hindu god, the eighth incarnation of Vishnu. His name derives from his dark complexion as the literal meaning of the word *krishna* is black. The Sanskrit root word of *krishna* also means attractive. Krishna, is depicted in various tales about him, as a charming individual who had a way of influencing everyone by his different qualities. The full incarnation followed a request from the gods and the Earth, all suffering due to the immense strength evil had come to acquire. He was the son of Vasudeva and Devaki. At various stages of his life, he is portrayed as a divine baby, a prankster of a boy, a model lover, a divine hero and finally the Supreme Being. He is the one whose dialogue with Arjuna in *Mahabharata* is the Geeta. He is the focus of numerous Bhakti (devotional) cults, which over the centuries have produced a wealth of religious poetry, music, and paintings. Besides, the *Mahabharata* he is mentioned in the *Harivamsha* and the Puranas especially the *Bhagavata-Purana*. (Purva Meghah XV)

Kunda (*Jasminum multiflorum*): Also known as Star Jasmine, it is an evergreen, branching vine that can be trained as a shrub, or as a spreading, vine-like shrub. It is one of the many forms of Jasmine found in India. It has very beautiful single-flowered, white blooms, which have no fragrance. The beauty of the flower more than makes up for its lack of fragrance. In Indian mythology the flower is used as a symbol of whiteness. So, instead of the common western phrase 'white as snow', what often appears in Hindu mythological stories is 'white as Kunda'. The single flowers appear in bunches, almost throughout the year. Laughter is also often compared to the white Kundas. (Purva Meghah LI, Uttara Meghah II, LVI)

Kurbaka (*Rhododendron arboreum*): Is the most widely distributed tree in the Himalayas. Called Laligurans in Nepal, it is the county's national flower. Of its many relatives, *Rhododendron arboreum* is the best-known and found in the Himalayan mountains from Kashmir in the west to Bhutan and Assam in the east. A robust tree, it grows up to 15 metres, has reddish-brown bark and bears blood red or pink to white flowers in clusters of about twenty in March-April. The oblong leaves, ten to twenty centimetre in length, are crowded towards the end of the branches. The flowers are used to treat diarrhoea and dysentery and its extracts applied to the forehead as a remedy for headache. The bark is used in the preparation of a snuff. It is also used as a hedge as the Yaksha tells the cloud while describing his home. (Uttara Meghah II, XVIII)

Kurukshetra: It was the name of the battlefield where the Great War mentioned in the epic *Mahabharata* was fought between the cousins Pandavas and the Kauravas. The place is said to have been named after king Kuru from whom both the Pandavas and Kauravas descended. At present, Kurukshetra is a town in Haryana State of India. Nearby is a place called Thanesar which some identify with the Kurukshetra of *Mahabharata*. Interestingly, the place has the remains of a fort the locals call Abhimanyu's (son of Arjuna) fort. (Purva Meghah LII)

Kutuja (*Wrightia antidysenterica* or *Holarrhena antidysenterica*): Also known as Kalinga, Indrayava in Sanskrit, Kurchi or Kuda in Hindi and White Angel or Snowflake Flower in English, it is a large shrub that grows up to five meters in height and is found throughout India in deciduous forests. It has medicinal properties and bears white fragrant flowers. (Purva Meghah IV, XXIV)

Lake Manas or Manasarovar: Is a freshwater lake located in Tibet which is of great religious significance to Hindus, Buddhists as well as Jains. According to Hindu religious scriptures, the lake was first created in the mind of Brahma, the Creator of the universe who along with Shiva, the Destroyer, and Vishnu the Keeper, is part of the Hindu triumvirate of gods. It is said to have manifested on earth later. The name is a combination of the words *manasa* (mind) and *sarovar* (lake). It symbolises purity, and along with Mount Kailasha is an important pilgrimage spot. Hindus believe that one who drinks water from the lake will be absolved of all sins accumulated over several lives. The water fowl that migrates to the lake at the commencement of the monsoons in India is believed to be Shiva's swan. The lake is very popular in Buddhist literature and associated with many teachings and stories in Buddhism. The Buddha, it is said stayed and meditated near this lake on several occasions. Jains associate Manasarovar with the first Tirthankar Rishabhdev. (Purva Meghah LXVI, XI, Uttara Meghah XVI)

Lodhara (*Symplocos racemosa Roxb*): It is a large evergreen shrub with gray-barked branches found in low-and mid-elevation forests from northern India to South-east Asia. It has elliptic rubbery leaves and cream white flowers borne in clusters, which give way to small, berry-like fruits that turn from green to purple-black as they mature. With well known medicinal properties since ancient times, it is also valuable as an ornamental plant. The bark contains compounds used in traditional medicines and dyes. The bark is used to prepare tonic for maintaining optimum health in women and a medicine for digestive disorders like diarrhoea. Its anti-allergic property makes it useful in allergic conditions and it is used internally as well as externally. (Uttara Meghah II)

Lord himself starts dancing: Refers to Shiva as Nataraja (king of dancers). See Mahakala (Purva Meghah XL)

Lord of Chandi and the three worlds: Shiva has been referred to by this name, as Chandi came out of the body of his consort, goddess Parvati. According to some of the Hindu scriptures, the gods, defeated and driven out of their abode by the demons Shumbha and Nishumbha, were praying to goddess Mahasaraswati for help when Parvati happened to hear their tale of woe. That was when Chandi or Chandika, described as a violent and impetuous form of the Supreme Goddess came into being from the form of Parvati. Though not mentioned in Vedic literature or the epics *Ramayana* and the *Mahabharata*, Chandi or Chandika is important in the Hindu pantheon. In her benevolent form, Chandi also known as Durga, one of the most popular folk deities in eastern India where Chandi is associated with good fortune as well as calamity. The three worlds refer to Heaven, Earth and Netherworld or Patalaloka. (Purva Meghah XXXVII)

Lord of riches: See god of riches (Purva Meghah VII)

Madhavi (*Hiptage benghalensis*): It is also known as Madhavilata or Atimukta and is a perennial, evergreen vine with white or yellowish hairs on the stem and long leaves native to India, Southeast Asia and the Philippines. Cultivated for its white-pink scented flowers, which bloom intermittently during the year, it can be trimmed to form a small tree or shrub or can be trained as a vine. It is also occasionally cultivated for medicinal purposes in the alternative Indian medicine practice Ayurveda. The leaves and bark are hot, acrid, bitter, insecticidal, vulnerary and useful in the treatment of biliousness, cough, burning sensation, thirst and inflammation. It also has the ability to treat skin diseases and leprosy. In stories of Krishna, Madhavilata is found everywhere in Vrindavana and creates a wonderful atmosphere with its fragrance and the three-coloured flowers. (Uttara Meghah XVIII)

Mahakala: Shiva is worshipped as Mahakala in Ujjain and it is third among the twelve most holy and auspicious of the 64 Jyotirlingas. Each one of the twelve Jyotirlingas takes the name of the presiding deity, each a different manifestation of Shiva. It is said that after Brahma created all the creatures and left them to live their lives, they became too numerous as they reproduced. Soon there were too many of them. Brahma wondered why. Then Saraswati pointed out to him that he had forgotten to create death. Realising his mistake, he created Mrityu (death) and ordered her to go about her job of killing creatures. Overawed at her task, Mrityu fled and was found by Shiva crying in a desolate place. He consoled and convinced her that death would not be the end of life but a gateway to a new one. So in handing out death, she would also be giving new life to creatures. Then Mrityu took the form of Mahakali and went about devouring all life. So Shiva became Mahakala, the Lord of Time, the Destroyer and Regenerator. According to the *Tantric* tradition (a form of yoga), Mahakala has four arms and three eyes, and is of the brilliance of 10,000,000 black fires of dissolution, dwells in the midst of eight cremation grounds amid vultures and jackals, is adorned with eight skulls, seated on five corpses, holding a trident, *damaru* (pellet drum), a sword and a *kharpa* in his hands. His body is covered with ashes from the cremation ground. Mahakali is of the form of the void, the dark space beautiful as well as fearsome and unfathomable. Shiva is the personification of time as Kala, and beyond the limitations of time as Mahakala. The cycle of birth, death and rebirth represent the temporal rhythm of existence which is seen as a great dance, and Shiva is depicted as Nataraja, the lord of dancers, the majestic cosmic dancer. The corpses under him symbolise human ego and ignorance. According to legend, Chandrasena the king of Ujjain was a devotee of Shiva. One day when he was praying, Shrikhar a farmer's son, heard his chants and tried to reach the temple to join the prayers but the king's soldiers caught him and took him away out of the city and left him on the banks of the Shipra. There he came to know of the plan of Chandrasena's rivals to attack the city and started praying for his monarch. The enemies enlisted the aid of the demon Dushana who could become invisible due to a boon granted by Brahma, attacked Ujjain and plundered it. They also attacked the devotees of Shiva as Dushana hated Shiva. Then Shiva appeared in the dreadful form of Mahakala and reduced Dushana and the enemies of Chandrasena to ashes. Realising that this form of Shiva was essential for peace in the world, the devotees requested him to reside in this form at Ujjain. That is how Mahakala came to reside there guaranteeing those who worship him in his Mahakala form freedom from the fear of death. (Purva Meghah XXXVIII)

Mala land: Is the ancient name of Malwa plateau region in the west-central part of India and north of the Vindhya range. Kalidasa, himself is said to have been based in Ujjain, which during the time of Avanti kingdom was the most important city of the area. Later, the region passed into the hands of the various dynasties like Mauryas, Kushanas, Shakas and Guptas. Under the Guptas, Ujjain flourished as a major centre of learning. After enjoying an independent status for sometime, it became part of Harsha's empire, and was later ruled by the Gurjars, Rashtrakutas and Paramaras. It saw a second intellectual flourish under king Bhoja before passing into the hands of the Delhi Sultanate which on break-up left the residual Malwa Sultanate among others. Thereafter, Mughals annexed it only to cede it after a while to the Marathas. The splintered princely states at a later date fell into the hands of the British Raj which created the Central India Agency. After India's independence in 1947, most of Malwa became part Madhya Bharat state and eventually Madhya Pradesh. Now Malwa corresponds to western Madhya Pradesh and parts of south-east Rajasthan. The plateau, with an average elevation of 500 metres is drained by Mahi river on the west, Chambal river in the centre and Betwa and others in the east. Shipra, Parbati, Gambhir and Choti Kali Sindh are other important rivers. The rainy season starts with the first showers of mid-June or Asadha (the time of year in which we find the Yaksha making his request to the cloud). Sambhar (*Cervus unicolour*) is one of the most common wild animals found in the region. Among the numerous tribes of the region are Bhils, Meenas and Kanjars all significantly different in their dialects and social life from the general population of the region. The Bhils have their own folk songs, including Heeda, anecdotal songs to the cattle, and the women sing the Chandrawali song, associated with Krishna's romance. These songs are accompanied by dance. The biggest festival of Malwa is the Simhastha Mela (fair), held every 12 years, in which more than 40 million pilgrims take a holy dip in Shipra river. (Purva Meghah XVI)

Malti (*Quisqualis indica*): Also known Madhumalti and the Chinese honeysuckle, it is a vine with fragrant 30 to 35 mm long tubular flowers that bloom in clusters and vary in colour from white to pink to red. Found in the wild in Asia and also cultivated, the vine can climb 2.5 meters to eight meters. In the wild it grows in thickets or secondary forests. The plant is used in herbal medicine. Decoctions of the root, seed or fruit can be used to expel parasitic worms or to alleviate diarrhoea. Fruit decoction can also be used for gargling. The fruits are also used to combat nephritis. Leaves can be used to relieve pain caused by fever. The roots are used to treat rheumatism. (Uttara Meghah XL)

Mandakini: It is mentioned as one of the transcendental rivers in the holy religious texts of Hinduism. Along with the Bhagirathi, Alaknanda, Dhauliganga, and Pindar it is one of the streams which join later on as they flow to form the Ganga. All these streams originate in the Himalayas in the Indian state of Uttarakhand. Mandakini is fed by Vasukiganga at Sonprayaga and joins Alaknanda at Rudraprayaga which then proceeds towards Devaprayaga where it joins Bhagirathi River to form the Ganga River. (Uttara Meghah VI)

Mandara (*Erythrina indica*): Also known as Parijata and called Indian coral tree or tiger claw in English, it is known for its strikingly beautiful flowers. It has spiny trunks and branches and is a species of *Erythrina* native to the tropical and subtropical regions of India and eastern Africa and some Indian Ocean as well as Pacific Ocean islands. It has large three-parted leaves that may be solid green or boldly patterned with bright yellow. In regions with a pronounced dry season, these fall once a year and are followed by beautiful scarlet blossoms. In India, the rich, red blooms make their striking appearance among the leafless branches in January-March. The short-lived flowers are quickly followed by the new leaves in early summer. A coral tree in full bloom is like an aviary. Crows, mynas, rosy-pastors, babblers and parakeets, as well as numerous bees and wasps swarm around to drink nectar, pollinating the trees. Soon after flowering, the big green pods begin to form. It has been widely used in Indian traditional medicine for treating common ailments such as asthma, arthritis, diarrhoea, fever, inflammation and leprosy. Its extracts have analgesic, anti-arthritic, anti-hypertriglyceridemia, anti-inflammatory and muscle relaxing effects. (Uttara Meghah VI, XI)

Mansions remain lit by the crescent moon on Shiva's head: A reference to the closeness of Alakapuri to Mount Kailasha, the abode of Shiva. (Purva Meghah VII)

Mount Kailasha: In Hindu mythology Mount Kailasha is the abode of Shiva, the Destroyer, who is part of the triumvirate of gods that includes Brahma the Creator and Vishnu the Keeper. Shiva, considered the destroyer of ignorance, illusions and ego is said to be meditating on that peak. He is shown sometimes alone, sometimes with his wife Parvati and at others with his entire family including sons Skanda or Kartikeya (also Murugan), Ganesha and their respective mounts the bull, the lion the peacock and the rat. The peak that lies close to Lake Manasarovar is also important to Buddhists and Jains. While its general location in Tibet is agreed upon, there are differences in opinion on the exact peak. Some say it is the one Tibetans call Khang-rin-poche, while others seek to identify it with Kiunlun range. While Hemkunta is mentioned as another name of Kailasha, a peak with this name is located in the Himalayas in the Indian state of Uttaranchal. Kalidasa refers to this as a mountain formed of crystals. Its peak has been hinted as covered with perpetual snow, serving as a mirror for celestial women and at another place it is said that Ravana loosened its roots in his bid to lift it. (Purva Meghah XI, LXII)

Nalagiri: It was the name of the royal tusker belonging to king Suppabuddha, the maternal uncle of Gautama Buddha, and father of Devadatta. Though jealous of the Buddha since his early days, Devadatta had joined the *Sangha* (Buddhist order) and in course of time developed some moderate supernatural powers too. According to legend, one day Devadatta went to Ajatashatru, the future monarch of the Magadha, and impressed him by his miracles so much that the latter became his devotee and patron. He now claimed superiority over the Buddha to assume the leadership of the *Sangha* by arguing that the latter had become old and senile. His claim, however, did not evoke much response in the *Sangha*. Spiteful, he plotted to kill the Buddha when he was in Rajgir (now in Bihar state of India). He got the huge tusker called Nalagiri intoxicated with alcohol, hurt and irritated, and let the enraged beast loose on a narrow street of Rajgir down which the Buddha was coming doing his alms round. The elephant started running down the street tearing down everything in sight. Everybody ran helter-skelter, but not the Buddha who calmed the animal with his loving kindness. The beast then bowed down at his feet with tears of gratitude running down his face. Tradition says that the Buddha had to encounter Nalagiri's wrath as a result of one of his evil *karmas* (deeds), perpetrated in one of his previous births when he, as a reckless haughty nobleman, had charged a Buddha by an elephant. However, Kalidasa here mentions Nalagiri roaming in Ujjaini. (Purva Meghah XXXV)

Nichai: Also referred to as Nicagiri, it has been identified by some scholars to be ancient name of the Udayagiri hills near Vidisha while others place it among the caves near Gwalior. (Purva Meghah XXVII)

Nipa: It is another name of Kadamba. (Uttara Meghah II)

Nirvindhya: It is a river now known as the Newaz or Newuj and is a tributary of the Chambal between Betwa and Kali Sindh rivers. It flows through Rajgarh, Madhya Pradesh. Kalidasa mentions Sindhu, Ganga and Brahmaputra as three great rivers systems of north India and Nirvindhya as a branch of the Ganga system. (Purva Meghah XXX)

Obedient to his overlord: Refers to Kubera. See Lord of riches (Purva Meghah III)

Overlord of gods: Refers to Indra the king of gods who rules from the *Swarga* (Heavens). He is also the god of rain and the *vajra* or thunderbolt is his weapon He is mentioned in the *Rigveda* as the one who has the supreme control over all horses, all chariots, all villages and all cattle, and also as the one who created the sun and the morning; one who controls the waters. (Purva Meghah VI)

Padma (Nelumbo nucifera): It is the flower of an aquatic plant considered sacred by the Hindus, Buddhists and Jains. Rising from roots that lie within the mud of a pool, the flower that blooms above the water in untainted beauty is considered the symbol of purity. Along with Shankha, it symbolises treasures and is one of the main attributes of Vishnu who holds

Shankha in his left upper hand, Sudarshana Chakra (discus), Gada (mace) and Padma (lotus flower) in his upper right, the lower left and lower right hands, respectively. The divine lotus is said to spring from the navel of Vishnu whilst he is in Yoga Nidra (yogic sleep). The lotus blooms uncovering the Creator god Brahma in Padmasana. It is also associated with Lakshmi and Saraswati. (Uttara Meghah XX)

Parashurama: Is the name of the sixth avatar of Vishnu who was born as son of Renuka and sage Jamadagni, one of the seven sages called Saptarisihi. A pupil of Shiva, he is described in the *Mahabharata* as the guru of Drona who later taught the Kaurava and Pandava princes, as well as of Karna, Kunti's first son born out of wedlock. An immortal despite being an incarnation, he is believed to be the guru who would teach the skills of warfare to Vishnu's last avatar Kalki whenever he appears in the future. Parashurama got his name, which means Rama with the *parashu* (axe), after he received martial arts training and an axe from Shiva himself on pleasing the latter with his penance. The most known story about him is that he rid the world of male Kshatriyas 21 times over (once for every time his mother beat her chest in mourning for Jamadagni) as they had become arrogant and oppressive on account of their power and one of them the Haihaya king Kartavirya had killed Jamadagni in order to take possession of his divine cow who alone had helped the sage host the king and his army. (Purva Meghah LXI)

Pradyota: King of Ujjaini. See Udayana. (Purva Meghah XXXV)

Prayaga: It is the ancient and still informally used name of Allahabad, a city in the Uttar Pradesh state of India. The name, which means the 'place of sacrifice', derives from the belief that this was the place where Brahma, the Creator, one of the three gods of the Hindu trinity performed 'yagna' to purify the atmosphere when he created the universe. This is the place where the invisible river Saraswati is believed to meet Ganga and Yamuna at their confluence. It has been called *tirtharaja* or the king of pilgrimages and there are a large number of places of religious significance in the city all having *tirtha* (place of pilgrimage) added to their names. Prayaga was the capital of the Kaushambi kingdom founded by the Kuru rulers of Hastinapur. Mughal emperor Akbar renamed Prayaga as Allahabad. (Purva Meghah LV)

Pushkara and Avartaka: Types of clouds. Pushkara also means blue lotus. It is also the name of a pilgrim town in India's Rajasthan state. Avartaka in the literal sense means recurring and seems to be an appellation for clouds as they do rounds gathering moisture and releasing it as rain. (Purva Meghah VI)

Rama: Is the name of the eldest son of king Dashratha of Ayodhya who was the seventh avatar or incarnation out of Vishnu's ten. He is described as Purushottama or the ideal man. Hindus believe that when the glory of Dharma or the path of righteousness is lost, Vishnu descends or incarnates on the earth in various forms to restore faith in righteousness by defeating the evil ones and unshackling his devotees from the cycle of birth and death. Satyuga or the age of virtue saw four incarnations of Vishnu, namely Matsya (fish), Kurma (tortoise), Varaha (boar), and Narasimha (man-lion). Vamana (dwarf), Parashurama (Rama with an axe, the ascetic warrior) and Ramachandra (the ideal man) appeared during the second yuga while the third age Dwapara saw the appearance of Krishna (the dark one who would not mind cutting corners to ensure the victory of good over evil). The last age in the cycle of ages, Kaliyuga or the dark-age (the present one), will towards its end see the tenth incarnation coming on a spotless white steed, which will be the Kalki avatar. That will be the end of the dark-age and then the cycle is supposed to restart with restoration of Sanatana Dharma (Eternal Religion, another name for Hinduism) and another Satyuga. Lakshmana the younger brother of Rama, Balarama the elder brother of Krishna or the Buddha are considered variously as the eighth or ninth avatars. Descriptions of Kalki also vary as does the very concept of the number of Vishnu's avatars with some putting the number at 24 or 25. (Purva Meghah XII)

Ramagiri Ashrama: It is believed that Ramagiri corresponds to modern day Ramtek city in the Nagpur district of Maharashtra. The Rama temple there is considered historic and it is believed by Rama stayed here when he was exiled from Ayodhya. The poet is talking about a hermitage there. (Purva Meghah I, Uttara Meghah XLIII)

Rantideva: Is the name of a monarch of ancient India who is said to have sacrificed so many animals including cows for feeding his guests (whom he considered the representatives of Vishnu) that the secretions from their skins heaped in his kitchen caused the formation of the river Charmawati or Chambal. That is why Kalidasa is telling the cloud to drink from the Charmawati's water as it is the result of sacrifices to the gods. He has been described as of rigid vows, always engaged in due performance of sacrifices, to whom countless animals, desirous of going to heaven, used to come. He is said to be the fourth in the generation after Bharadwaja and given to offering whatever he had to guests, himself undergoing considerable hardship along with his family. A story about his devotion of Vishnu tells that whenever Rantideva was of service to anyone, he would feel that it was a service to the god. Vishnu also considered him his greatest devotee. But this was questioned by other gods. When Indra asked him who his favourite devotee was, Vishnu named Rantideva, the son of Sankriti as the one. Brahma and Indra and other gods like Vayu and Varuna decided to test Rantideva. So suddenly unseasonal rains and winds destroyed the crops and his country was overtaken by famine. Rantideva used his granary and treasury to keep his people fed but crops kept failing. Rantideva gave up his palace and all his belongings to keep his people away from hunger, but misfortune would not go away. He even gave all his food to the people. He fasted and prayed to Vishnu for forty-eight days to protect his people when his worried ministers convinced him to break his fast. Just as Rantideva was about to eat, a hungry man came and the king handed over a portion of his food to him. When he again sat down to eat the left over food, another hungry man came along and the king handed over another portion of his food to him. The third time yet another hungry man came along with his as hungry dogs and the king handed over the remaining the food to them. Then again, when he was about to drink the water, the only thing left, a thirsty Chandala (someone who deals with disposal of corpses) appeared. The king handed over the water to him as he too was the creation of Vishnu and the king saw the god in him. That was when all the gods appeared and told him that the three men and the dogs were they in disguise and the Chandala was Yama (the god of death) himself. They had found what Vishnu said about Rantideva to be true. Everything that was taken away from Rantideva's people was restored and he was granted *moksha* (salvation) by Vishnu and merged into him. In another version of the tale, Maya (illusion) appears ahead of the Chandala and offers him all sorts of riches should he pray to her. But the devotee of Vishnu declines what she has to offer because he is absorbed in Sri Hari or Vishnu. (Purva Meghah XLIX)

Ravana: Is described in the *Ramayana* as the demon king of the fabled city of Lanka who kidnapped Rama's wife Sita. Son of sage Vishrava (also the father of Kubera) and Kaikesi, he had Mandodari, the daughter of Mayasura, as his wife. He is also said to have been an able administrator, great warrior and as great a scholar. Also called Dashanana (one who has ten heads), he had a boon from Brahma according to which, he would be killed only by if the Amrita (nectar) in his navel is removed. His ten heads are said by some to symbolise his immense hold on diverse branches of knowledge like astrology, statecraft and medicine, and by others, different emotions. To secure the boon of immortality from Brahma, he cut off his 10 heads one after the other as a sacrifice and in the end succeeded in getting the nectar instead. He also sought invincibility against all beings but humans whom he considered too weak to be of any harm. After getting the boon, he usurped Lanka from Kubera. Then he went to meet Shiva and had a tiff with his bull Nandi. In his arrogance, he even attempted to uproot and move Mount Kailasha, irritating Shiva. Later, he realised his folly and was able to please the god gaining the divine sword Chandrahaas from him as a gift, though with a caveat not to use it for unjust purposes. He is said to have composed the hymn known as *Shiva Tandava Stotram*. Thus strengthened, he dominated the heavens, the earth and the netherworld and became the emperor. In the *Bhagawata Purana*, Ravana and his brother, Kumbhakarna were said to be reincarnations of Jaya and Vijaya, gatekeepers of Vaikuntha, the abode of Vishnu, who were cursed to be born on earth. They had the option to live seven lives as normal mortals and devotees of Vishnu, or three as powerful enemies of Vishnu. Eager to return, they chose the latter and were born as Hiranyakashipu and Hiranyaksha, Ravana and Kumbhakarna and Dantavakra and Shishupala to be slain by the Narasimha, Rama and Krishna incarnations of Vishnu respectively. According to another story, Ravana was smitten by the beauty of Vedavati who was performing austerities to win Vishnu as her husband. He proposed to her and when she rejected it he tried to use force. She burnt herself to death saying she would be born again to cause destruction. It was Vedavati who was born again as Sita, and was the moving cause of Ravana's death, though Rama was the agent. (Purva Meghah LXII)

Reva: It is one of the names of the Narmada river. While Narmada means the giver of joy and befits the river's beauty, the Puranic name Reva comes from its other attribute which is the rapid leaping movement of its water due to the rocky bed on which it flows. It is one of the five holy rivers of India along with Ganga, Yamuna, Godavari and Kaveri. It is the only river whose circumambulation is considered a pilgrimage by the Hindus and its over 1,000 kilometre length forms the traditional boundary between north and south India. Interestingly, the river's valley, inhabited since Stone Age but guarded by the difficult Vindhya and Satpura mountain ranges along its length for a long time, has enjoyed a somewhat demographic and cultural distinctiveness. (Purva Meghah XX, XXI)

Rewati: Was the wife of Balarama and the only daughter of king Kakudmi of Kusasthali whose realm lay under the sea. When she grew up into an exceptionally beautiful woman (Kalidasa mentions the intoxication of her eyes) her father could not bring himself to marry her to a mere human. So he went with her to the place of Brahma to seek his advice on the matter. While he was there for a short celestial while, ages had flown past on the earth (a day and night of Brahma, according to Hindu belief are equal to 8.64 billion human years) and the king's contemporaries and their sons and grandsons had passed away. When told about this, the king was astonished and Brahma amused at the astonishment. Brahma then told Kakudmi about Vishnu's incarnation as Krishna and his elder brother Balarama, and suggested the latter's name as a groom for Rewati. Back on earth, they found human beings had become smaller physically and intellectually so Rewati was far bigger in stature than Balarama. Balarama brought her to a stature befitting the age before marrying her. (Purva Meghah LIII)

Sagara's sons: The allusion to king Sagara refers to the death in ignominy of his sixty thousand sons as they had insulted Kapila, the sage. They were, however, absolved of their sins because of the penances of Bhagiratha (see Ganga), his great great grandson, as he succeeded in bringing Ganga down on earth from heaven. The river water washed their ashes. (Purva Meghah LIV)

Saraswati: Is the name of a river mentioned in Hindu scriptures as one of the three rivers along with Ganga and Yamuna meeting at Prayaga (Allahabad) in a holy confluence called Triveni. Rising in the Himalayas, it was said to flow south-west. According to earlier texts like *Rigveda*, its course lay between the Yamuna and Sutlej but later on, having dried up in a desert, it is said to be invisible. The river was identified with the goddess of learning Saraswati. A number of efforts have been made to identify the river with various scholars holding different opinions. For some, it was the same as the one now known in one part of its course as Ghaggar and in the other as Hakra, while for others, it was the Helmand River of southern Afghanistan. There are still others who in their bid to identify the river have sought to look at the underground water channels that run under the Thar Desert parallel to the Aravalli ranges. Not withstanding the scientific efforts and differences of informed opinion, the belief that the river flows underground to meet Yamuna and Ganga at Prayaga creating Triveni, the three-way confluence, holds. (Purva Meghah LIII)

Sarika (Gracula religiosa): Also known as the Hill Myna is a medium-sized gregarious passerine bird. Native to southern Asia, especially north India, their preferred habitat is fairly open country, and they eat insects and fruit. Plumage is typically dark, often brown, although some species have yellow head ornaments. They live around human habitation, and are effectively omnivores. Hill Mynas are considered talking birds, for their ability to reproduce sounds, including human speech, when in captivity. In Hindu tales, Myna is described as a female bird while the parrot is the male bird and often they are attributed the faculty of human speech. (Uttara Meghah XXV)

Serpent bed: It refers to Shesha or Adishesha, the king of snakes and one of the primal beings of creation on whose coils Vishnu is seen reclining in the middle of the primordial ocean with Lakshmi sitting at his feet. (Uttara Meghah LIII)

Shankha: Is a conch shell derived from a species of large predatory sea snail (*Turbinella pyrum*) which lives in the Indian Ocean. It is of religious significance in Hinduism as well as Buddhism and used as a trumpet in religious rituals and war. In Hinduism, the Shankha is a sacred emblem of Vishnu, the Preserver, and considered a giver of fame, longevity and prosperity. Perhaps, that is why it is painted on the door of the Yaksha's house along with the Padma (lotus), another attribute of Vishnu. The reverberations of the sound it produces represent the primordial sound Om. In ancient times, it was also used as a war trumpet and the sound it made is called *shankhanad*. It is also the cleanser of sin and the symbolic abode of Lakshmi, the goddess of wealth and consort of Vishnu. As a symbol of water, it is associated with female fertility. Shankha is used in Ayurvedic medicinal formulations to treat many ailments. In Buddhism, it is one of the eight auspicious symbols, also called Ashtamangala. (Uttara Meghah XX)

Sharabha: Is a mythical animal mentioned in the Indian scriptures as having eight legs. Sometimes it is described as an eight-legged deer and at others as a beast which is part-lion, part-bird, part human and more powerful and ferocious than a lion. It can jump across a valley in one leap. Sharabha is also said to be an incarnation of Shiva which tamed Vishnu's fierce man-lion avatar, Narasimha, which after killing Hiranyakashipu and drinking his blood, became troublesome on account of his inability to digest the gore. Vaishnavas however hold that Sharabha is another name of Vishnu. In Buddhism, Sharabha appears in Jataka tales as a previous birth of the Buddha or a bodhisattva. In *Mahabharata*, Sharabha, is mentioned as residing on Mount Krauncha as an ordinary beast. The epic also includes Sharabha as an edible mriga (deer) which could be Sambhar (*Cervus unicolour*). This appears to be what Kalidasa is referring to in the poem. (Purva Meghah LVIII)

Shipra: Also written as Kshipra, which means pure, is one of the holy rivers of India. It originates in the Vindhya ranges in Madhya Pradesh state and flows north across the Malwa plateau to meet the Chambal. The ancient and holy city of Ujjain is situated on the right bank of the river where the Simhastha Kumbh Mela (fair) is held every 12 years. The hermitage of sage Sandipani where Krishna received his education was situated on the bank of Shipra. The river is said to have originated from the heart of the Varaha, the boar incarnation of Vishnu. According to another story, it originated from the blood flowing out of Vishnu's finger which was chopped off by an angry Shiva when the former pointed it at him. (Purva Meghah XXXIII)

Shiva: Along with Brahma the Creator of the world and Vishnu the Preserver, Shiva the Destroyer forms the trinity of Hinduism. He is also the supreme yogi. He has forms both benevolent and fearsome. As the Destroyer he is responsible for change. The crescent moon on his head, which gives him the name Chandrashekhara, is one of his ornaments. It notable that though the moon's waxing and waning is the basis of the lunar calendar used by the Hindus, it is only an ornament as Shiva himself is Kala or Time. As Nataraja he is performs the cosmic dance Tandava (see also Mahakala) which has the creative Ananda Tandava as well destructive Rudra Tandava forms. The rhythm of this dance represents the cyclic time. (Purva Meghah VII, XXXVIII, XLVIII, LIV, LX, LXII, LXIV, Uttara Meghah XIV)

Shiva's Bull: Named Nandi, he is the bull which serves as the mount of Shiva. He guards the gate of his master's abode Kailasha and accordingly is found outside Shiva temples (in earlier temples Mahakala is the other guard). Puranas say Nandi was born out of the right side of Shiva in his own image and was given as a son to the sage Salankayana. He is also mentioned as the son of the sage Silada who got him by the grace of Shiva. According to a legends, when Shiva drank the sticky *halahala* the poison (said to represent human karma or deeds) that came out after the churning of the ocean which no one else could digest, Parvati stopped it in his throat (that is why Shiva is called Neelkantha or the one with a blue throat that came to be so due to the impact of the poison). Some poison, however, fell out of his mouth and Nandi drank it to prevent its disastrous impact on the world. All present there, gods and demons alike, were worried for Nandi but nothing happened to him, since having completely surrendered to Shiva, he had all powers, abilities and protection of Shiva himself. Nandi was the one who cursed Ravana that his kingdom would be burnt by a Vanara (monkey). He is also the chief guru of the 18 Siddhas or masters of arts and sciences. (Purva Meghah LVI, Uttara Meghah LVI)

Siddha: Siddhas have been described as "certain semi-divine beings noted for their purity." The attribution of naivete to Siddha women and the later reference to pairs of Siddhas with their lutes (considered by commentators as mildly suggestive of the erotic) suggest that the poet had such beings, or alternatively, simple forest dwellers, perhaps, a tribe of the time, in mind. More well-known are the Siddha saints, proponents of a vast body of knowledge including everything from grammar to medicine, and practitioners thereof. While the Siddha tradition has its roots in north India, it merged with and branched off into a separate Siddhar tradition in the south especially Tamil Nadu, with sage Agastya, a migrant from the north, being considered the first one of that tradition. The presence of such Siddhas in those parts of central India, where the cloud's journey begins, and further west, is mentioned in other sources. The mention of Shiva worship by Siddhas who are also linked to Shaiva Siddhanta would also suggest that Kalidasa was talking about these Siddhas. At the literal and most basic level the word *siddha* refers to someone who has attained perfection in a particular field as also to the expertise itself. Also, in the *Mahabharata* where the illustrious Ashtavakra's journey is mentioned, it is said that moving northwards, he reached the Himvanta Mountains peopled by Siddhas and Charanas. (Purva Meghah XIV, XXIII, XLIX, L, LIX)

Sindhu: It refers to Kali Sindh river, one of the main perennial streams of Malwa region fed by Parwan, Niwaj and Ahu rivers. It has its origin in the Vindhya Range in Dewas district of Madhya Pradesh from where it flows northwards, through the Jhalawar and Baran districts of Rajasthan meeting the Chambal in Baran district. It belongs to the Ganga basin. It is referred to as Dakshina Sindhu in the *Mahabharata*. (Purva Meghah XXXI)

Sita: It is the name of the consort of the Hindu god Rama (incarnation of Vishnu) and is an incarnation of Lakshmi, the goddess of wealth and consort of Vishnu. She is esteemed as a standard-setter for wifely and womanly virtues for all Hindu women. Having come out of earth, she was the adopted daughter of king Janaka of Mithila and Queen Sunayna. In *Ramayana*, towards the end, she descends back into the earth from where she was found by Janaka during a ceremonial ploughing of the field. (Uttara Meghah XLII)

Skanda: One of the two sons of Shiva, he is the warrior god who leads the army of the gods and has peacock as his mount. According to scriptures, Shiva withdrew from the world and engaged himself in yogic meditation in the Himalayas after Sati immolated herself stung by the disrespect shown by her father king Daksha towards Shiva. (Before withdrawing he flew into a rage and created havoc but was calmed down through Vishnu's intervention.) The withdrawal left the gods in a fix as only the son of Shiva could defeat the demons Surapadman and Tarakasur. To get around the problem, the gods sought the help of Kamadeva, the god of desire, to make Shiva fall in love with Parvati (the reincarnation of Sati). But the disturbed Shiva, who would love no one after Sati, opened his third eye and Kama was immediately reduced to ashes. While the gods' plan to get Shiva marry Parvati fell into disarray, his fiery emanation due to the intervention of Kamadeva underwent three stages of gestation within the flame of Agni the fire god, water of the river Ganga (refer to Kalidasa's reference of Ganga as a playful maiden) who was also unable to sustain them, and the six Krittikas (the stars that make up the Pleiades cluster) finally to be found in a reed forest as six children and raised by the six Krittikas, earning the name Kartikeya. Parvati combined these six babies into one with six faces (Skanda is also called Shanmukha and Arumugan both of which mean one with six faces) who as a youth (Kumara), became the supreme general of the gods and lead them to victory against Surapadman, Tarakasur and others. Surapadman saved himself by agreeing to become the mount (peacock) of Skanda. Thus Skanda is in a way the self-begotten son of Shiva. In ancient times, Skanda used to be worshiped in northern India where there are still a few temples devoted to him but now he is an important deity in the south. The caves at Ellora and Elephanta have images of Skanda. In Buddhism, Skanda is regarded as a devoted guardian and a bodhisattva, Vajrapani who wields *vajra* or thunderbolt in his hand, and is the commander in chief. He symbolises the ability to protect his devotees from evil influences and effects through love, compassion and understanding. (Purva Meghah XLVII, XLVIII, XLIX)

Son of the Wind: The epithet refers to Hanuman a Hindu deity, who was an ardent devotee of Rama. Hanuman is mentioned as an avatar of Shiva or Rudra in the Sanskrit texts and was the son of Anjana, an Apsara cursed to be born as a monkey and Kesari, after the couple performed intense prayers to Shiva to get a child. According to a story, when Anjana was worshipping Shiva, king Dasharatha of Ayodhya was also performing a penances for having children. The prasada (portion of offerings) he received was to be shared by his three wives. A kite snatched a part of the prasada and dropped it near Anjana. Vayu, the Hindu deity of the wind, caught it before it fell to the ground and delivered it into the outstretched hands of Anjana, who consumed it leading to the birth of Hanuman. So he is also called the son of Vayu while still being considered as an incarnation of Rudra (Shiva). He is a central character in the epic *Ramayana* and also finds mention in several other texts, including *Mahabharata*, the various Puranas and some Jain texts. Hanuman is worshipped by villagers as a boundary guardian, by Shaiva ascetics as a yogi, and by wrestlers for his strength. (Uttara Meghah XLII)

Tala (*Borassus flabellifer*): It is one of the varieties of the Palmyra palm also known as toddy palm and is native to South and Southeast Asia. It can live over 100 years, reach over twenty meters in height and has tough fan-shaped leaves that are upto two meters long. The leaves were used for writing in ancient India. Highly respected in Tamil culture, it is referred to as Kalpavriksha (wish fulfilling tree) because all its parts without exception have a use. (Purva Meghah XXXV)

The Great War: It refers to the war at Kurukshetra fought between the Pandavas and the Kauravas which is the subject of the epic *Mahabharata,* the longest epic of the world. (Purva Meghah LIII)

Three-quartered stretch of sleeping time: As per traditional Hindu time keeping, a day is divided into prahars or pahars of three hours each. So there are eight prahars. The Yaksha's reference to three prahars of sleeping time is thus equivalent to nine hours. (Uttara Meghah LI)

Tripura: In Hindu mythology it was the name of three Asura (demon) brothers, the sons of Tarakasur. The brothers (Vidyunmali, Tarakaksha and Viryavana), after defeating the gods, ruled the world from their three fort cities of gold, silver and iron located in Heaven, Sky and on Earth respectively due to a boon given by Brahma, the Creator. The boon also laid down the condition that after a thousand years the forts would become one (also Tripura, as the word means three cities) and the three brothers would die only if someone destroyed it with a single arrow. Shiva achieved the feat after the gods pleaded with him to do so and that is why she is also known as Tripurari (foe of Tripura). The victory is celebrated on Kartika Purnima the full moon day of November-December which is the fifteenth lunar day of Kartika month as per the Hindu calendar and is also called Tripurari Purnima. According to one interpretation of the story, the three fortresses symbolise ego, deed and illusion, which tend to drag the soul (*atman*) away from god (*paramatman*) by creating a false sense of being. Shiva the Destroyer is the only one who can free the individual from them. (Purva Meghah LX)

Udayana: He was a powerful Vatsa king who ruled Kaushambi, which had a running strife with the more powerful southern neighbour Ujjaini, ruled by Pradyota. Young, handsome, and highly accomplished, Udayana was a popular king who also had the ability to tame elephants, wild as well as those trained for war, by playing music on *veena*. Once, when Pradyota's army attacked Kaushambi, Udayana used the skill to calm the former's war elephants. Realising Udayana could not be defeated in battle due to this skill, Pradyota wanted to learn it. Meanwhile, Yaugandharayana the wise minister of Udayana wanted the two warring states to make peace. If Udayana married Pradyota's young, beautiful and talented daughter Vasavadatta that end could be achieved. Now one day, Udayana got the news that a white elephant was grazing in the forests on the borders of Kaushambi. Tempted to catch the rare elephant, he went there with his *veena*, Pradyota's soldiers, waiting in the vicinity, captured him and brought him to Ujjaini. Pradyota told Udayana to teach him the wonderful art if he wanted to be released. The latter agreed with the rider that Pradyota would have to accept Udayana as his guru (a teacher, as per custom, has a higher status and is to be respected by the pupil). Pradyota would not do that and instead decided to get Vasavadatta learn the art from Udayana. But he was afraid that the two, young and attractive as both were, might fall in love. So Udayana was told that he would be teaching the art to an ugly hunch-backed girl in the family and would be separated from her by a curtain. Similarly, Vasavadatta was told that the teacher was a leper. One day while learning, Vasavadatta was repeatedly making the same mistake. Udayana lost patience and called her hunch-back. An incensed Vasavadatta sought to remind him that he himself was a leper and added he had no idea who she was and also that he had no right to call her such names. Shocked, Udayana pulled away the curtain. The two fell in love immediately. Yaugandharayana's mole appeared on the scene in the nick of time and helped the two escape to Kaushambi and marry. Pradyota had to accept his daughter's choice and the two states became friendly. (Purva Meghah XXXII)

Ujjain: Is a city situated on the bank of the river Shipra in Madhya Pradesh. Being the capital of the ancient Avanti (one of the four great powers along with Vatsa, Kosala and Magadha) kingdom, it was also known by that name. Earliest mentioned as Avantika in the time of Gautama Buddha, the city is referred to as of Ozene in the Periplus of the Erythraean Sea, an antique Greek description of sea ports and trade centres in the western Indian Ocean. The city believed to be ruled by Mahakala (Shiva as Lord of Time and also Lord of death), has been a religious and cultural centre in India since ancient times. The prime meridian of the Hindu calendar since the fourth century BC passes through Ujjain. It is believed that the location of Mahakala defines the Shankuyantra, an important instrument in Indian astronomical calculations. The *swayambhu* (born of itself) Mahakala is one of the twelve Jyotirlingas and the only one facing south, making it very important to the tantric tradition. The temple renovated by successive dynasties including Shunga, Kushana, Satavahana, Gupta, Parihar, Parmara was pulled down by Altutmish but reconstructed later. Mahakala worship by Vikramaditya and Bhoja is well known and the temple used to receive royal grants for *puja* (worship) expenses even in the Mughal period. The city saw rulers like Chandragupta II, scholars like Brahmagupta and Bhaskaracharya, and literary gems like Kalidasa. It is regarded as one of the seven sacred cities (Sapta Puri) of the Hindus. It is one of the four sites that host the Kumbh Mela (also called the Simhastha Mela). It is said that after Sagar Manthan (churning of the primordial ocean to discover the pot of nectar) when *amrita* (nectar) was discovered, the gods and the demons fought for it as it would bestow to immortality. In the process, one drop fell on Ujjain (also on Haridwar, Prayaga and Nasik), thus making the city immortal and sacred. (Purva Meghah XXIX)

Vaibhraja: The fabled garden of Kubera (Uttara Meghah X)

Vatsa: Considered an offshoot of the Kuru clan, which traced its lineage to kings Puru and Bharata, the Vatsas had their kingdom located around the present day Allahabad in Uttar Pradesh state. Their capital Kaushambi was a prosperous city and an important gateway for goods and people travelling between north-west and south. Udayana was a powerful Vatsa king who later adopted Buddhism as the religion of his kingdom. (Purva Meghah XXXV)

Vetrawati: The name means 'One full of reeds'. Now known Betwa, the river originates in Madhya Pradesh state of central India. Flowing northeast from its origin in the Vindhya mountain ranges it merges into the Yamuna near Hamirpur in Uttar Pradesh. The roughly 600 km river runs half its course over the Malwa plateau and the other half in the Bundelkhand uplands. While itself a tributary of the Yamuna, Betwa has Jamni and Dhasan as its main tributaries. The river finds ample mention in the ancient epics like the *Mahabharata* and mythological texts as Vetrawati and Suktimati. (Purva Meghah XXVI)

Vidisha: It is a city, about 75 km north-east of Bhopal between Betwa and Bes rivers, was known as Bhilsa till 1956 when it was renamed for being close to ancient Vidisha. The Vidisha which finds mention as Besnagar in Pali scriptures is three kilometres from the present Vidisha. It was a busy commercial centre during the time of the Maurya Sunga, Naga, Satavahana and Gupta rulers and declined before rising again as Bhilsa during the medieval period under the sultans of Malwa and Mughals before passing on to the Scindias. Emperor Ashoka was the governor of Vidisha before ascending the throne after his father's death. (Purva Meghah XXVI, XXXII)

Vindhya: It is one of the major mountain ranges of India which is about 1,000 km long and extends from Mirzapur in Uttar Pradesh through Madhya Pradesh and Rajasthan to eastern

Gujarat and along with Narmada has been a traditional dividing line between north and south India. Amarkantak is its highest point while Narmada, Kali Sindh, Parbati, Betwa, Ken, Son, Tamsa or Tons rivers originate in the range. The Aravalli range lies to its north west and Satpura range runs parallel to it in the south. It is older than the Himalayas and on the plateau north of it lie the cities of Bhopal, the capital of Madhya Pradesh and Indore. It is said that the Vindhya had such a tendency to grow that it was becoming so big and arrogant as to obstruct the path of Surya the sun god and even demand that the later should change his route. So sage Agastya journeyed south and on reaching Vindhya asked him for a way to let him cross and continue his travel. Vindhya bent low to let the sage cross and agreed not to gain height till his return. Agastya never returned and the awaiting Vindhya never grew further. (Purva Meghah XX)

Vishnu: Is the name of the second god in the Hindu triumvirate (or Trimurti) that includes Brahma and Shiva. He is the Preserver and Protector of the universe. His role is to return to the earth in troubled times and restore the supremacy of good over evil. So far, he has been incarnated nine times, but Hindus believe that he will be reincarnated one last time close to the end of this cycle of time. Vishnu is portrayed as blue or black skinned and has four arms. He has a thousand names and chanting them is an act of devotion. In the Vedas, Vishnu is ranked among the lesser gods and is usually associated with the major Vedic god Indra who in the epics and Puranas is shown fights against demonic forces. (Purva Meghah L, LXI, Uttara Meghah LIII)

Wish fulfilling/granting tree: See Kalpa tree. (Uttara Meghah XV)

Yaksha: In Indian mythology the Yakshas are demigods. They have Kubera, the god of wealth as their king and are tasked with protecting his treasures and gardens. The suffering protagonist of *The Meghaduta* is an attendant of Kubera. (Purva Meghah I, VII, Uttara Meghah IV, V)

Yamuna: Also known as Kalindi and Yami, Yamuna originates in the Banderpooch peaks of the Himalayan ranges from the glacier called Yamunotri. Chambal, Sindh, Betwa and Ken are among the tributaries of the river which itself is the largest tributary of the Ganga. It meets the latter at Prayaga (Allahabad) after flowing over 1,300 kilometres along with the invisible Saraswati at Triveni Sangam. Between them, the two rivers create the highly fertile alluvial, Yamuna-Ganga Doab. A bath at the confluence is considered very meritorious and a Kumbha Mela (fair) is held there every 12 years. The coming together of the two rivers is visible as the water of the Ganga is white while that of the Yamuna is black. This is what Kalidasa is referring to when he talks about the reflection of the dark cloud in the Ganga. In Hindu mythology, Yamuna is daughter of Surya (sun god), and twin sister of Yama, the god of death. While a dip Ganga, the epitome of asceticism and higher knowledge grants *moksha* or liberation, a bath in Yamuna, symbol of love and compassion grants freedom from the fear of death the charge of her brother Yama. The river finds wide mention in the religious texts and epics. The capital of Pandavas, Indraprastha, was located by the Yamuna while there are a host of associations with Krishna. According to another Puranic tale, stricken by the arrow of Kamadeva, Shiva became restless and to cool himself, he jumped into the Yamuna causing the water turn black. (Purva Meghah LV)